C U T

ADAM CUSHMAN

Cut

a novel by **Adam Cushman**

ISBN: 978-1-7353646-0-5

BURNT TONGUE BOOKS

First Edition, July 2020

10 9 8 7 6 5 4 3 2 1

Previously published in paperback by
Black Mountain Press, 2014

Library of Congress Control Number: 2020912492

Printed in the United States of America

Cover Design: Damonza

Author Photo: Sylvain Caron

PUBLISHER'S NOTE

This is a work of fiction. Names, characters, places, and incidents are either the product of the author's imagination or are used fictitiously.

"...and you shall know the pleasure, constantly renewed, of escaping from yourself to forget yourself in another being, and of attracting to yourself other souls to lose themselves in yours."

**—Charles Baudelaire,
from Paris Spleen**

For Alexandra

1

TERMINAL

You find your seat in the tail section, jam your bag in the foot space, buckle tight and pull some hair out of your arm, then a few strands from your eyebrow.

You don't do this because it hurts.

You do this because you're nervous and afraid of dying.

You think airplanes seem like they're getting bigger every few years, while the elbow-room narrows, stuffing us like a more civilized version of how we used to ship slaves.

It's a five-hour flight from Burbank to MIA and Amistad Airlines charges ten big ones for in-flight meals.

The flight attendant gives you this information with a mouthful of whites and sparkly blue California eyes.

You are absolutely positive her expression would be the same if she'd come over to tell you that you had a terminal disease, or that your girlfriend was stabbed to death in an SUV, along with three of your closest friends.

What if you don't have ten dollars, you want Carol to explain. Five hours can last a lifetime when all you've had since you left your motel room in North Hollywood is a Redline and stale peanuts.

Things you would never consider putting in your mouth seem all of a sudden desirable and worth exploring.

You imagine the boat ride to the new world, lying on one of those slippery slabs covered in essential fluids, staring straight up at the back of someone's head for six months.

Could be your girlfriend or your sister lying next to you, and before too long, you might snap one of their necks and chew your way through just to breathe.

Some food for thought, but what you think you would do, you'd never do it like you're thinking.

Besides, how can it be murder if you don't mean it, if there was never any choice, except choosing between them?

Is it so hard to accept that when it comes down to it, you might love yourself more than them, or others more than some?

You pull a crumpled up ten out of your pocket and unfold it. Someone's written *Anything to Wake Up* in red ink. You press the help me button and Carol brings your food.

You stab the last bite of chicken between your cheeks as the captain says to prepare for the initial approach into the Miami area and not to turn on our cell phones until we've landed and begun taxiing, because if we turn on our phones, we will cause a mid-air explosion.

If we think about turning on our phones, we will

cause a mid-air explosion and if we think about a mid-air explosion, survival is imminent, and all of these things are fine, because you haven't turned on your phone in over five months.

On your lap lives a small pile of brown hair you pulled out of your hands, arms and head strand by strand just before takeoff and during some unexpected turbulence.

It's not always stress-related.

Sometimes it's mindless, other times you do this in your sleep, and more often than not, it's just really fucking stimulating, kind of like the juicy popping sound when you pull your eyelid by the lashes.

You live for that sound.

When you step out of the gate, you're running on fumes.

You hit the bathroom and while you're washing the airplane off your hands, you gaze in the mirror at the crusty, chapped-pink-under-the-eyes guy with bushy brows and doughy muscles you've become.

Your clothes are a baggy T-shirt and cargos as always.

On your left arm shines a tattoo of Harriet Tubman waving a pistol.

Over your shoulder you carry an orange duffel with some college football team's faded emblem.

Your fellow cabin-mates continue deplaning with the same proud, chin-high glare.

Some rush for the yogurt kiosk, some step onto the moving walkway and stand on display, others stop to watch twenty-four-hour news channels on their way to baggage claim, heads cocked upwards, a laptop bag in one hand and peanut crumbs falling off their peach-colored golf shirts.

They don't see you standing in front of the pay phone closest to the water fountain, watching them watch with careful concern like the newscast airs with them in mind.

You're waiting for a phone call.

They told you to stand in this spot for further instructions.

Right now it's one-thirty-something in the AM and you're in a noisy claustrophobic airport that smells like a wet dog in a brand new car.

You tell yourself it's about keeping things in motion. You tell yourself it's about not stepping backwards. The phone rings and your hand braces the chipped receiver. You reach up, twist and pull and before you know it, there's a tiny bird's nest in your palm that you shake off from between your fingers and watch as it floats downward.

You were such a nice boy when you were younger, at least that's what your grandparents used to say when they saw you turning into a weirdo.

A weirdo trying to be an actor, trying to be other people, the kind of people who always make the right choices.

Your future was supposed to be different from this twisted mess that gets more tangled every time you try to unravel things.

You could try your sister, who's probably calling your cell phone from another airport in God-knows-where, but why stick the blade back in both of your wounds?

The ringing gets louder and even though there's more

than enough hair on your body to wait it out, you asked for this.

You're fresh out of excuses. Go ahead. Do it. Come on, you gutless loser. You big faker.

This phone call could make all the pain go away if you'd just slip out of your brain and let it save you.

This could be your big break.

2

THE BEAK

"HE MAY SEEM preachy at first," the man's voice tells me, "That's just how he says hello."

The man on the phone says to wait for the short skinny dude wearing the wife-beater.

He says he's blond with thick black eyebrows because he'd gone and colored his hair.

The humidity hits me once I'm curbside at arrivals, wayward hairs sticking to my skin.

After placing my bag down and rolling a cigarette, I spot someone in jeans and a windbreaker scooping garbage by the taxi stand.

It's sad and amazing because she's the kind of flawless, doe-eyed brunette who volunteers at the Vet's office, Candystripes, and makes love.

Only she's a street sweeper.

"Let me help you," the old me would say and go home all prune-faced.

Besides, she probably sticks with the job because guys

mess with her all the time, tell her she's too pretty to be doing what she's doing and does she want to take a ride.

Maybe she's an actress headed to LA.

Maybe she wants to earn her way like ugly people.

Maybe holding on to the pain keeps her in character, or makes her nobody at all.

Track three from the *Shaving Under Your Eyes* album blasts from a green mini-van as it pulls up alongside me.

I wave at the street sweeper. She empties the scooper into the trash bin.

The Beak wolfs down the rest of a burger, balls up the wrapper and unlocks the passenger door.

The Beak wears long silver chains from his belt loop that clink together when he moves like self-imposed shackles.

The thick eyebrows could have easily been applied with a Sharpie.

His dyed-blond hair seems more orange, and because he looks semi- Hispanic, Jewish, or Italian, this makes him seem like a five-foot-six cartoon version of himself.

The Beak has a sweet manner that contradicts the street vernacular. This is the kid who called his friends' moms ma'am.

Before the questions begin, we're passing through Coral Gables onto US-1 as I pull stubble hairs from my chin and slip them in my mouth.

At a stoplight at Kendall Drive, a short black guy in a torn Member's Only jacket and no shirt punches a white kid as they walk down the sidewalk, punches him hard in the back of the head saying, "Give me a mother fucking job, man."

The guy he's punching is young and tan, wearing shorts and carrying a bundled up T-shirt in his hand.

Sometimes there's a secret pleasure in seeing people more screwed up than ourselves, a hint of relief, how behind the false sympathy and that crumpled-up dollar we never dig out, we're glad to be us.

The Beak tells me his vitals: Miami: born, raised, and broken. Now he's a company man. The Artful Dodger of swampland.

"You mind the music? Want me to change it?"

The new car smell is giving me a headache in my eye. I glance and see the rear-facing baby seat and an unopened box of wipes.

"Got a three-month-old baby girl," he says and grabs a creased picture from atop the visor, "Check it. Beautiful, right?"

He hands me an overexposed four-by-six of a shriveled thumb with a face.

"Nine-pounder," The Beak says as he takes the photo back, tells me, "That there's my little angel. We even named her Angel. Me and the wife closed on our crib last month, two-story in the Palmetto area. Pretty safe, which is cool too, whatever that means, you know. I guess it's a tract house and all that, but it's about what you do with the inside, right? That's where the freedom's at."

I conjure up the image of a prolapsed rectum as the strip malls and wet air whoosh past my window.

"You don't mind I'm driving fast, do you?"

The smell of his wife's mall perfume, the fast food bag and the cherry air freshener hanging from the rearview, all these things are making my temple throb.

"You're nervous, ain't you?" He puts his hand on my knee and with a reassuring laugh that's not very reassuring explains, "You're cool, man. Just kick back and take a deep breath. The Beak'll get you all straightened out."

Coffin size. Burial arrangements. Last rites. All straightened out. Why do people say this or say, "Let's get something straight," or "Don't worry, I'll straighten up this mess?" This is part of the problem.

Not everything's supposed to be straight.

Without some kind raveling, everything will continue to be in tangles the straighter we try and make it.

Pretty soon, rows of stucco homes fill the windshield.

"Where we're going, this is America. The little guy always wins, you know what I'm saying? Even if he loses, he still wins."

We pull into a cul-de-sac on a residential street somewhere in West Kendall. Cars line the pie-shaped driveway.

We park and with a quick flip of the wrist he turns down the music and looks at me with his mouth open in the shape of an o, like he's whistling and nothing is coming out.

I should have known better than to get in a van.

He says, "Saw you checking out the street sweeper. She's a cold-blooded killer, you know? What I heard from one of the ladies be hanging out near the airport underpass. Watch out for a ho called Agnes."

"I got Agnes pegged for a man."

The Beak smiles and moves his head back and forth.

"Well some people are crazy like that," I say.

"Yeah?"

"Not my kind of crazy, though."

"You sure? You got that crazy look. You coming here makes you some kind of crazy."

"There's all kinds of crazy," I say.

The Beak unsnaps his seatbelt. "Just thought you might want to let go of some of all that tension."

This would be a good time to tell him that tension so works for me.

The Beak kills the engine and opens his door, which, for some reason that's supposed to be technologically amazing, doesn't make a sound.

"I could be anyone," I say.

The Beak's grin widens to reveal one jagged, fanged front tooth among flawless whites.

"You got a point. You could be a cop. You could also be a dude who six years ago took a road trip to the Keys from the University of West Virginia, you and your sister and a bunch of college kids. Could be you picked up a stranger named Ronald Coleman who went all Tex Watson, and well, all kindsa crazy, all you had to do was pick up the local paper, read about how only you and your sister made it out alive. Point is, we know your smelly, lonesome ass plenty good. Now follow me, actor boy."

3

THE LIVING ROOM

THE BEAK RINGS the bell and a guy with a giant forehead, tight and shiny opens up.

His beady yellow eyes smile when my throat contracts.

The Beak says, "This here's all kindsa crazy," and winks at me before introducing me to Kuba, who raises a pistol, and gestures down the hall toward two double doors.

Once inside, the Beak tells me how Kuba's some weird mix of Chinese and Irish and is only here for a few weeks before he goes back to Chad to finish his degree in giraffe philosophy or some shit.

When we reach the double doors, The Beak tells me, "There's three things can happen to a dude that overnight changes how he looks at shit: We all know the first one is pussy. Second is knowing everyone you love is gonna die."

"What's behind door number three?"

"If you ain't ready for what you came all this way to do, if you got folks somewhere who give a fuck if you live or if you don't: Walk out this place and forget. 'Cause when you wake up tomorrow, you ain't gonna be the same skinny dude who came out that SUV six years ago with all them stab wounds."

The Beak says, "You sure you ready to do that again?"

With a thumbnail, I squeeze out a few hairs from my moustache and almost tell The Beak getting stabbed in the stomach, arms and thigh was the greatest thing that ever happened to me, and all I want to do is repeat it.

"All right, brother," he says, "Here's to falling forward."

He turns the knob to the sounds of overlapping voices.

Navajo-white living room walls and a Chinese rug under a micro-suede sectional.

The fireplace lights up with a switch and the king-sized plastic tarp falls over the room.

A plasma's mounted on the wall, watching us.

A group of five sit slouched against the farthest side and could be home- less children.

They're the locals camped outside a tattoo shop on Venice Beach, or the record store clerks on St. Marks Place.

The carved guy in the denim jacket sees me and sinks his chin to his chest.

The Beak leans in, "That there's Fred. All kindsa crazy, just like you."

Fred's grinning at me. He has large ears.

The Beak says, "Fred's been stabbed over thirty times. Dude next to him with all those animal tattoos is Wonkie. Real name's Juaquin. He's a different kind of crazy. Next to him's Bam Bam, Pebbles, and the smelly freak with the beard at the end is Alex."

The Beak half-points at the sliding glass door to the back yard.

On the other side waits a slender black girl, a curl of smoke climbing the sides of her cheeks as she faces the screened-in porch.

"That's Comfort," he tells me, "Least that's what she calls herself."

Comfort's wearing jeans and a black T-shirt with the sleeves rolled up just below her shoulders.

"This here's anyone's bet," he says as we sit on the sectional. "The kid's never done this shit before. Comfort just bounced back from a gut wound."

Before I can ask, a kid comes out of the dining room.

He's wearing swim shorts, Elevation X sneakers, and a long-sleeve T- shirt with a rabbit, which he removes and tosses on the floor before stepping onto the tarp and stretching his hamstrings.

White sunspots cover his pimply, athletic back.

Comfort enters and takes a position next to the kid on the tarp.

A gray-haired man comes out of the kitchen eating a hard-boiled egg, dressed in a tracksuit and glasses.

Tracksuit places a Canon 5D on a tripod next to the couch, frames the shot and presses record.

Something about the Beak not mentioning the man in the tracksuit tells me we're in his house.

Comfort's black eyes dart around at every little movement. Maybe the credit card debt spun out of control. Student loans. Overdrafts.

Late car payments.

Or maybe she's hoping to lose.

Peeking from behind the table with the Swarovski crystal ducks, I swear Coleman's watching me with dog eyes, same fishing shirt he wore that night in the Keys, running his fingers through his beard and licking his chops.

"You wanna take her place, don't you? What about the kid though? Don't he deserve to keep his life?"

The Beak leans in too close, his face getting red.

"Remember one thing: That girl you thinking can't really wanna do this shit has as much a chance as anyone. Think about something else: If it was you in the middle of the living room, would you be trying to save her life then and if the answer's yes, you need to tighten up quick or take your ass back to wherever town it is you living in this week 'cause homes, you ain't gonna make it."

The ambience is heavy breathing and an occasional clearing of the throat.

Kuba comes out of the kitchen with two long knives and hands one to Comfort, one to the Kid.

The Kid laughs and says something to Comfort, who says nothing.

Fred and his circle whisper.

A tiny pink-haired girl sits among them, Pebbles is rail-tie thin, with giant lips and eyes, like if an extraterrestrial were kind of hot.

Pebbles watches the Kid like he's about to burst into fire as Bam Bam wraps his arms around her waist.

The other orphans wouldn't look any different if they were watching a mayonnaise commercial.

Tracksuit turns the stereo up with his remote and starts the soundtrack to some movie I can't remember.

Comfort and the Kid step away from each other as The Beak whispers something in Tracksuit's ear.

Fred and the others wait for it.

Tracksuit says action and Comfort flies at the kid, swipes the blade at his chest.

He recoils in time, turns the handle around and shields his face with his other hand as he circles her.

Comfort follows with her eyes. The Kid orbits her a second time. The slightest of smiles. He laughs when her knife enters his side.

Comfort's out the sliding glass door with a cigarette lit seconds after he hits the floor.

The kid gushes.

Tracksuit kneels, takes his hand.

"The pain is temporary, son. The freedom you've just attained, that's forever."

The kid smiles as his eyes roll back and a Middle-Eastern man in a leather jacket enters, takes his pulse and snaps at Kuba.

Kuba carries the kid away and the man follows them into the kitchen.

"Where are they going?" I ask.

The Beak starts texting.

He says, "The kitchen. That Iraqi dude is a world-class surgeon. Best excuse me now, I got to get to Publix before my wife goes apeshit."

The Beak leans in, but I have to bend down because he's much shorter than me.

"You're smart, I can tell," he says, "one of those quiet

types. I respect that, son. Bet you know without me saying nothing that you committed the second we walked in. So you might want to pick up a blade."

Here's me stepping toward the glass door, over the pool of blood leakage trying for a closer look at Comfort.

A figure moves behind me, removes his denim jacket. Fred rests a gentle hand on my shoulder. "Would you think it was so sad if she were fat and sloppy?"

"By the way," he whispers, "That guy you're so relieved didn't stab your little honey smack's name is William, and William almost paid for a semester of community college in forty seconds."

"How many people have died in this living room?"

"It didn't start out like this," he says, "You've arrived at the end, you just don't know it yet."

Fred takes the palm of my hand, flexing his grip from dead-fish to bone- cracker and back again.

"There's a bus stop in front of the pleasure palace you're staying at. See you there at noon."

I notice Tracksuit at the front door, whispering to a man in a real suit, a black man who straightens his tie, scratches his moustache and picks up a silver briefcase, both of them seeing me watching them before the man in the suit exits.

Fred says Tracksuit is Mr. Lopez, and the black man's name is The Handle. He says they make all this happen.

Lopez shuts the door, smiles wide and shoots me with his finger.

I press my face against the sliding glass door, staring at the back of Comfort's head as cigarette smoke curls above her shoulder.

4

NOCTURNE

ON MY CAB ride back to the airport underpass to see if the street sweeper's still sweeping garbage, I for some reason remember her with Comfort's eyes.

Then I'm back where I started and there's no street sweeper, or anyone else until there is.

"Got a light for me, sugar?" asks a voice behind me.

Pull back to reveal a black woman wearing a shrunken Atlanta Falcons jersey and leather gloves even though it's hotter than shit.

She smacks a pack of menthols on her palm, walking in place, like it's freezing outside.

She hasn't made eye contact yet as she digs in her jeans and finds some matches, tells me, "Never mind, baby," and lights up. "My name's Agnes. Why you got hair all over your shirt, sugar? You sure as hale ain't been shaving."

I glance around one more time for the streetsweeper, then lean in and ask, "What's the ten-minute-rate for a fresh-off-the-boat type to hold you around back, nothing else?"

"Shit, baby," she says, blowing minty smoke, "How much you got?" When she sees the change come out of my pocket she looks away.

"Just a little?" I say.

She takes a drag and studies me.

I'm whispering, "Right here is fine."

"You know, I got a little secret might make you think twice…"

"I don't care," I say a little too loud.

The seventy-eight cents flies out of my hand.

I scoop up what's around me.

"I don't even care who you are right now."

The way Agnes stares at the ground tells the brief story of me not having any human contact.

"I got one more semester at the Gonzalez Massage School and my ass is certified. You take care now, sugar. Remember, Jesus forgives. Even you."

Agnes stamps out her half-smoked cigarette with the heel of her boot and meanders next to a metal fence.

Watching her mosey over to the bus stop without a glance, I chew off a chunk of my hang nail, then wait for it to bleed.

Think of this as a little pick me up.

Jesus forgives.

Even you.

5

CICELY

THE BATHROOM AT the High Palms motel is orange with Rorshach-shaped stains in the basin.

You wash the sleep from your mouth, throw on your cargos, grab your Army jacket from the duffel, and put on your prayer face.

The alarm clock's missing pieces of digital numbers, so you bless the power button on your hell phone and it rings immediately.

"Gabe where the *fuck* are you?"

"I'm in a cop bar in Pacoima. No, wait, an energy healer's flat in Durango. Shit, wrong again, I'm sitting in a Church pew in Altus, Oklahoma."

"Where are you really?"

"Praying for us sinners. Tell me, will you know the hour of His arrival or are you prepared to walk blindly into the mouth of Hades?"

"Are you doing your lame ass theater crap again?" She means the method.

Becoming someone else entirely.

Full immersion.

You used to do this for days on end.

Even though there was no play you were ever cast in, no lines to remember.

You did it because being anyone was better than being you.

So you'd wake up and start acting. Acting like you weren't yourself today.

"Pull your head out of your ass, loser, I've been calling your stupid phone for five months," a sad little pause, before she gets all dignified, "I just flew in to Long Beach. I had a layover in Hartsfield last night. Before that, Boise."

"Busy, busy girl. People clearly depend on you."

Here's the thing about Cicely: ever since six years ago, she's been jumping on random airplanes.

She never hangs out in any of the cities, just sleeps in airports, gets on standby lists and flies to the next airport.

She says the airport remains the most meditative place on Earth.

She says the airport is a place of detachment, of the between, and that she's a citizen of the world in perpetual transit.

The whole Buddhist thing has poisoned her mind. Mao was right.

"Cic', something happened last night and it's changed me."

"What's her name this time?" she says, which is darling.

She's alluding to the old you again, who would wake

up in heaving sweats over a random girl who grazed your arm at the bookstore, or scanned your frozen pizzas.

Until you crawled out of the SUV. Still, this is Cicely's way of saying you're a numb bastard while also reminding you why, as if you might have forgotten what happened to the only girl who ever fawned in return.

Cicely's saying, "I didn't mean that."

You ignore it and tell your sister, "This is something extraordinary."

From three thousand miles away, her dramatic sigh still turns your stomach into a pretzel.

"Well are you going to tell me, or what?"

"Sorry. Can't do it."

"Why not?"

"You have to ask me."

"Ask you what?"

"Ask me how, Cicely."

"I'm asking. Okay?"

"Are you prepared to accept Captain Jesus as your ..."

"I'm hanging up," she cuts you off, even though she can't, because she doesn't have anybody else to listen to her bullshit.

She says, "Why do you have to mock everything that's important to me? Sometimes I wish you'd just kill yourself finally."

"Then who'd talk to you?"

"I believe in being a better fucking person."

A slight pause, then, "You've been misled."

"At least I'm trying not to be miserable. You're the embodiment of Dukkha."

She's referring to her cult again. You thumbed through

that stupid book she sent you last Christmas. The verdict: Fuck Tibet. Fuck beads and fuck dream catchers. None of that shit makes people spiritual. It makes people assholes.

"Listen to me. There are no Chakras, Noble Truisms, Scatmans or happy fat people. Cicely. Understand something: Eternal fire..."

"I'm throwing this phone in the trash in two seconds you skinny, pasty, lonely piece of shit."

"Cicely? Sweetheart? I'm not lonely. Not anymore."

"Die already!"

"I'm trying. But we're twins, remember? Whatever bounces off me..."

"Suck a fart out of my ass. At least I... Shit, TSA's coming, I have to blaze. Call me, okay?"

"It might not be too late."

"You better call me, Gabriel. I'm seri..."

Click.

The clock on the phone says it's almost noon.

You're sweating again, peeling on your socks and sneakers, the vein in your forehead thick as a pencil.

6

ROLL CAMERA

"I'M GONNA TALK about Jesus!"

Late risers scowl, snort, and lock eyes with their news-papers. My head feels like it's touching the roof of the metro bus. "I said I'm gonna talk about *Jeeeeeeeeeesussssah!*"

"All you people. Yeah. Every day you drink your coffee and read your paper, throw it in the garbage. What does that tell you? Huh? You're putting garbage in your head!"

My eyes scan the frozen faces lined in rows of seats and back benches.

The black man in the suit clenching his jaw, the old lady with the turkey neck, and the Chinese kid wear-ing the red Computer Universe work shirt, his acne in constellations, all have the ability to ignore sensory dis-turbances down to a science.

"Don't mind my pacing. Look not with your eyes as the Captain gives unto you eternal life."

Fred's sitting at the back of the bus with his arms

folded, a sports bag filled with two phone books he asked me to bring and a bottle of kerosene on his lap.

Some Hindi chick in a tank top has kept ogling him since I got on board and found his all-enlightened-looking ass sitting in silent meditation, except to send me hell-fire glares.

Dark fuzz in sideburn formation that isn't a beard of course, because she's a girl, yet otherwise kind of is.

Fred eyeballs her.

She's rubbing her prickly thighs.

Heading south on Kendall Drive toward the Everglades, me and Fred haven't exchanged a word since I handed him the greater Miami white pages and went about my business.

Sweat stings my eyes as a mom with one in the stroller and another bun baking rolls her kid away from me.

Phase two of this exercise is getting in people's faces and breathing the Lord into their mouths in passing.

"Blessed are the poor in spirit, for theirs is the kingdom of heaven."

The black man in the suit shoots out of his seat, brandishing a moustache and a finger in my face.

He whispers, "I will murder you."

Deep down, I'm screaming for this guy to cold clock me into silence, as I have now become the creep on any given bus ride who I'd normally be the heavyweight champion of disregarding.

Instead he falls back into his seat and stares at the ground.

With flecks of spit flying in faces, I'm yelling, "Behold. My soul hath not been polluted."

Maybe it's the empty black eyes or the headphones, but my legs won't let me move beyond the Chinese kid.

Over his shoulder, the bearded girl is now sitting beside Fred, both of them watching me.

Her head's buried in the shoulder of his denim jacket like they've been sick with love for months.

Sometimes you just have to slap the Jesus into people.

"May the glory of heaven shine down and seize us!"

The slap makes the whole bus jolt. My palm stings upon shouting, "Hallelujah! Let the Almighty reigneth!"

The bus screeches to a stop at Krome Avenue because there's a gun in my face.

Token gasps and blasphemies all around before my new Chinese friend cocks the hammer and says, "Pick up my headphones, bitch!"

I comply.

He tosses them on his seat and steps to me.

"You fucked up, didn't you?"

My throat contracts as the driver exits the bus, along with the suit and a few up front.

"Why you ain't praying, bitch?"

A bullet in the forehead feels long overdue, but there's something about staring down the barrel of a nine-millimeter that makes my fucked-upness suddenly tolerable, and worth clinging to.

Cic', bless her vagabond heart, might say that there is no gun, not really.

She would insist there is nothing that exudes "gunness" about what's pressed against my forehead.

"Bitch what's wrong with you, you deaf? I said pray."

She would say, "Point to the gun," and I would and

25

she'd chuckle, telling me, "You're pointing at a point on the gun, not the gun itself, therefore, that thing you call a gun has no intrinsic reality, so it is not harmful to you in any way."

"You praying? Pray, bitch! Pray, punk! If your brain's still in your head in five seconds, there's your miracle."

Cic' tells me, "This idea of emptiness is how that monk in the '60's set himself on fire without feeling a thing."

For some reason, me telling my sister, "Get fucked, you hooker," comes out of my mouth.

His finite smile makes his weapon a cold hard fact, any spot you point to.

Fred's bony hand touches my shoulder, saddling my back-peddle as he says, "Hey, Arthur," and this is when the first sign of life appears in my executioner's eyes.

Arthur's jaw slackens.

"You're friends with this asshole?" I'm saying.

The muzzle on my forehead hasn't moved.

Fred tells Arthur, "Everyone knows you miss him, brother, but none of this brings him back."

"Motherfucker," a winded laugh with the promise of tears, "I know you or something?"

"No. No, not really. But I know you a little. Like how you're twenty- three and won't move out of your mom's house because you can't take the guilt. I also know you play the keyboard kind of decent, but better if you'd lay off the meth and stay away from the skating rink parking lot with your boys on weekends. I know you paid retail for that Colt, you hate being Thai, and you think no white girl is ever gonna love you."

The bus has been drained save a few souls in back.

"Thai, Arthur? I'm the first one to get it right in years aren't I?"

Fred removes a wad of cash from his jacket pocket tied together with a red rubber band and holds it out.

"This what you want?" he says, "Take it."

He says, "Go buy your mom that reclining mattress she's been seeing on television. Or better yet, get her car fixed so she doesn't have to sit around all day."

Arthur, eyes on the money, says, "How you know so much about my mom, man?"

"Bang," I'm saying, pounding my chest, then yelling, "Bang, bang, bang," and Arthur's lips purse when he swats my finger from his forehead.

Fred's saying, "I want to buy this man's life. I need him on this side of the grave a few more days. Go ahead, take the money. It's a lot."

"This ain't about your money. Set that shit on fire all I care."

Arthur presses the barrel harder against my forehead.

Fred raises an eyebrow in my direction, says, "All right," throws his cash on the ground, douses it in kerosene, and strikes a match."

"Yo, I was just messing, don't— Yo, what's wrong with— I'll end this mother fucker."

Two gutsy passengers brush past the flames, leaving turkey neck and Fred's new girlfriend.

The smell of dead president's screams chases the aborted down the aisle.

"See," he's telling Arthur, leaning in now, saying in a private manner, "Nobody likes being slapped. Especially you. Truth is, I'm a hundred percent you don't have the balls for this."

"You do not wanna say that shit to me."

"Things like, 'Pull the trigger, you Dyslexic virgin?'"

"Shut up. Shut the fuck up. This is a gun, fool."

I say, "Arthur, I don't know him. I just talked to him one time at a knife fight."

Fred bounces back, "That's a lie, Arthur, we've been like *this* since we were kids. Now he's found God and slaps people all the time, gets me in all kinds of shit worse than this. Open him up. Do us all a favor."

"You think I won't?"

"Look at his Army jacket. Semper Fi? Look in his eyes. You're all Japs to him."

Turkey lady in the back stifles her sobs.

Between the gun burrowing through my skin, and wanting to stab Fred in the neck, something makes one of the dull brown vessels in my left eye sizzle and pop, which confirms whatever truth Arthur needs to hear.

Click.

Arthur scowls at the gun, pointing it at his own face.

"Conversely," Fred throws in, "Certain pistols of the Colt/Browning type will unlock when pressed against a human body," then whispers, "That means they won't fire, in case you're confused."

The bus is one big sweat drip, including the passengers on the tips of their toes outside.

"All right, all right. Question: Are you still gonna blow my friend's mind away for bitch-slapping your dumb ass or are you maybe gonna stop acting like the

cliché you are and do something, like for starters dropping that piece of shit Colt off at Goodwill?"

Maybe this is the scene in the movie where Arthur's
lips quiver and he has a moment of clarity so he puts the
gun down and falls weeping into Fred's arms as the rest
of the passengers applaud.

Cue the sad symphonic music and prepare my relieved
close-up before we all puke in unison, right?

Here's the alternate ending:

Arthur says, "I'mma hang on to it."

Fred knocks me down with a clothesline and arches
his back thirty degrees before the first shot, which takes
out the back window.

High-pitched ringing and the second and third shots
are direct hits, one to the gut, one to the heart, as from
the floor, my back putting out the financial bonfire, I
catch the last of Arthur sprinting out the double doors,
along with the split-second thrill in his nickel-gleamed
eyes as Fred crashes on top of me, flushed of color and
sucking for air.

Fred's bearded bride screams like her hand has been
lopped off.

She pulls at him and turns him on his side as his hacks
and coughs remain bloodless.

A wan smile forms as the last words of a dying man
follow painful, scratchy laughter.

Fred's saying, "Pray for us now at the hour of our
death."

7

BABOONS WITH HAMMERS

Cicely always says when someone dies, no one should touch the body for three days.

She says bodies won't decay as quickly if they're left to settle, because the person's energy has time to disengage.

When people perform CPR, move the body, and poke around, this can mess up what happens to the dead person, like if they'll return as a hamster, a person again, or move up.

My sister talks about cases where the body was left alone and rigor mortis didn't set in for a week.

She says this also depends how far along on the eight-fold-path the dead person was.

I tell her when I go, just do the usual.

I say I'm lucky to come back as somebody's ball hair.

But sure. Some dead people maybe you should leave alone.

Fred and me are several miles deep in the sweltering Everglades.

Gretchen, Fred's new girlfriend, claims she's pre-med at FIU and is sitting shotgun in our new bus, AC blasting, her face buried in a portable Nintendo she lifted from an abandoned backpack.

"Twelve-hundred-dollar vest and would you look at these bruises. My surgeon's going to be so pissed."

The purple thing on Fred's stomach is worse than a bruise.

The chest welt is smaller, but bleeds a little from the center, the puncture of a pin to a prune.

He lets the vest dangle on his finger.

"Here's to Arthur for not opting defense rounds." Tossing the vest he says, "Poor kid saved my life in his own way," then winks and grabs two Seal knives out of his bag.

"Careful," he says, throwing me one that takes a few fumbles to catch. I notice the satin finish and medieval ridges. The padded grip feels terrific. Which explains the handshake last night in the living room.

"Made her this morning, should be a custom fit.

He's saying, "Don't lose it. That's a hundred-and-four-teen-dollar knife. Here. Tape this to your chest."

Fred heaves a phone book and a roll of duct tape over each shoulder, sending me into a swamp puddle to intercept.

I slide the blade between my teeth and pick at the tape to come off the roll.

Here's the thing: The Homestead white pages are not as thick as the greater Miami phone book.

Over there we're talking five or six inches, much

thicker than the pamphlet I'm strapping on, not to mention, they've been dumping corpses out here for decades.

While we baja'd the bus through fauna and mangroves, I saw a human leg sticking out of the swamp.

Fred holds up his blade, tells me, "Shirt off, companero."

The way the sun bounces off my new amigo's chest creating beams of white light in four directions makes him difficult not to look at, not because the man is carved out of hairless stone and not because of the perpetual loose smile that makes me need his friendship, not even close, it's the constellation of knife scars that orbit his body, varying in color from white as dice to shades of violet.

"There are thirty-six, not including the tattoo or the exit wounds," he says, chin lowered, making final adjustments.

"Tattoo of a what, a knife wound?"

"Try and guess which one. Nobody can."

With one hand pressing pages L-Z firmly to his chest, Fred wraps four layers of tape around and rips without letting go of his blade.

In an attempt to pull my shirt off with some sort of swiftness, my arm gets tangled behind my head and I'm forced to drop the phone book.

"Wow," he says, "You're like a girl with hair. Dig this, it's all those fast food hormones made your nipples the size of silver-dollar pancakes."

"He looks closer at me, "Is that Harriet Tubman?"

I clear my throat before sucking in my gut as I wonder

why Mr. Observant hasn't noted the scars on my chest and sides from Coleman's blade.

Scars just like his.

Scratching the top of his head with his knife handle tells me Fred is ready.

"Give me a second." The tape sticks to my arm hair as I try to reach around without dropping the phone book.

"Take your time, Nipples, we've got fifteen-to-twenty before Homestead PD accesses the bus's AVL system and gets a description of the perp."

The perp being me, the guy who peeled out in the bus. Asshole's idea, but he really seemed almost dead at the moment.

"Think I got it," I say.

My head slams against the trunk of a Bald Cypress.

Everything goes white and under my tongue gets fuzzy.

When my breath comes back, Fred stands over me, pointing to my midsection as he pulls his blade out of the phone book hanging from my chest.

"Nicely done," he says, then becomes narrow-eyed and concerned as my palms meet at the nape of my chin, the pleas exiting my mouth in quick whispers.

Anything to wake up.

"Man, you are a wicked strange dude. What are you? Failed actor? Your girlfriend die?" He smiles.

I take his hand and a great force lands me on two feet.

"How do you know so much about people? How'd you know all those things about Arthur?"

He back-steps and hurls the blade in a wind-up pitch.

Fast forward to me face-first in the marsh, minus the fuzzy feelings and bright-whiteness.

"You're not very good at this."

A spitful of crabgrass as I grab my blade and jab it a few times in his direction, like poking the air's going to knock him over.

"What are you doing?"

"Hating your guts."

"Reverse your grip. Point the edge out and hold it up in your fist. Now rake downward, and try to slash across my face."

I step toward him and rake. Fred clasps my forearm with his free hand and releases. "A lower tier of retarded." The thing about trying to stab people is when you've never hurt a living thing, there's a hurricane of sensations.

Your face gets heavy, both hands shake and your scrotum falls asleep.

Cic' would say these are your chakras telling you to quit it.

"Stop thinking about your life. Become one with that thing."

My fist clenches around the handle and my elbow juts out in my full state of knifeness.

Fred doesn't blink as I swing too high, slicing air.

"Try again. Relax your grip and imagine the blade going through me. You're leaning in for the first kiss. Once you go for it, it becomes all about confidence and chemistry."

Deep breath in. Be the blade. Be yourself, being the blade. Be everyone you've ever seen being the blade.

Be the Justins with their peanut butter skin and curious neckties, brandishing cell phones hip-side like incompetent cowboys with the occasional goatee and espresso stride, be Merediths, skirted corporate-casuals boasting egg-breath power lunches, sitcom get-togethers and cogged lingo made of strewn together words such as *detail-oriented.*

Forward-thinking.

Consumer-ratio.

Be Tims and Erics who wear faded ball caps and fraternity rape smiles in their throats.

Deep breath out, and steady.

Heathers, Kristens, Jills and Taras, bleach-blonde, spaghetti-strapped, tattoos of Indian relics on the smalls of their backs, sipping green beer through fluorescent twisty straws and whistling Christian rock in topless jeeps.

Christian rock. Piety masquerading in sin's garments.

None of these people ever see me. One slap would get everyone's attention. "Got a minute for Jesus?"

The time is now. Be the blade.

There's my knife wedged in his phone book. Fred's mouthing something good. Oh God. Here it comes... Fast forward.

Here's Fred in close up. I don't recall collapsing, but feel lighter somehow. There goes the airplane chicken. Nice brown drool string. We're live in five, four, three...

"Everyone pukes the first time," and he lifts me up one-handed.

He takes a few pulls to tear away his phone book, spins the pages of names until the last paper slash, and says, "Muy bueno, cabron. You got all the way to X. Two letters short of my thirty-seventh wound."

Then he slaps me on the arm, slaps Harriet, brings me close, locking foreheads.

Fred's saying, "We might just be great friends."

He looks at his watch, one of those rubber 1980's models with the calculator.

"Brace yourself," Fred tells me, then he thrusts the blade into me, deep into the pages, and the tip entering a millimeter past the surface of my skin tells me this one went somewhere beyond Kaufman, Jeffrey.

Another spitful of wet grass as I twist my head up and back to see Fred's warm smile descending, the *Tiny Farm in the Country* dad from TV, before the Chemo, safe and secure in the fatherly gaze.

Cue the warm fuzzy family music and spread your butt cheeks. I'm asking if Fred was the one who trained Comfort.

"What happened to her?"

"I agree with you, the world's a great big pile of doody," he says.

"Here it is," he says. "You're not allowed to put your knife down until you fight next week. You sleep, eat, shit, bathe and spank it with that thing glued to your hand. If I see you without it at any point under any circumstances I'll just start stabbing you. Capice?"

He heads toward the bus as the oily mirage of a crappy green pick- up truck moves toward us, one male silhouette inside, Icelandic dirge rock blazing.

Gretchen's leaning against the door, leering at me, her eyes big and her mouth open with the teeth of a shark.

On my knees, I stretch the skin on my stomach with two sets of fingers.

So maybe it didn't break the surface or rupture a kidney, but this heat is poisonous, an alligator just slithered into the sawgrass, and for the first time since the last one stopped, there's a girl breathing who's twisting my guts like wet rags, making me question everything.

Such as why I started sending emails when I saw the video of two guys knife fighting in the living room all those months ago.

Some homicidal girl that's never seen my face has that kind of power.

Cic' would say I'm being my typically obsessive self and that people who obsess over stuff can never be spiritual, or truly free.

8

THE CAMERAS OF GREED

TRACK FIVE FROM *Shaving Under Your Eyes* means these
headphones see your souls and know whether you're it.

You live down here long enough, all you see is that
crack head look.

See red lines in their eyes snap crackle from OD'ing
on iPhone screens, stripmalls, and wanting shit.

People here, they're easy to figure.

You don't even have to be no kind a hustler, just show
a little common sense, say to yourself, "What they after?
How am I gonna make them think I can give it to them?"

I learned that shit working for the big North Miami
Beach hotels, knowing folks' life story from fifty yards,
lugging their ugly-ass clothes in black bags from cabs and
stretched limos to rooms with pink Jacuzzis, knowing
what the tip's finna be soon as they step out the car.

Dude gives me five bucks he's got this look says he
done saved my life with kindness.

And he expect me to make sure everything's cool for

him now, extra special treatment now 'cause he ain't come here to fuck around sure enough.

All this back before I got a real job.

This job.

Part of which is walking up Collins Avenue waiting for the right fish and bait the mo'fucka.

But knowing who to hook makes this easy, makes this doing whoever his or her lucky-ass is I take with me a favor they ain't never gonna forget.

Some folks, a knife is the best thing ever gonna happen to them.

Take this dude over here, fat ass hairy shoulders bitch in the tank top, roly poly biggums, gonna have to oil his ass just to get him in the room.

He's hanging with three skinny dudes he go to the University of Miami with, and dress how they do and talk how they do and he do whatever the fuck they throw at him, maybe, "Yo, Jabba, go get us a cab," or, "Yo yo yo, piggy, take your ass inside and grab us some beers or some shit,' and he smiles and he do it 'cause he ain't never been cool before, ain't never had friends who weren't spanking it to comic books or who didn't wear a retainer till they was twenty-five.

He'd do anything to make his ass look smooth in front of these fools, these jeep-driving rapists with their lawyer pop's trust fund.

Now they're standing by the fountain outside the Clevelander, talking shit to all these fine-ass bitches who ain't never gonna even think about fucking them 'cause they got no rap and no game, ain't got no manners neither.

And fatty don't say shit, but he smiles and laughs and sips his beer every eight seconds.

Just gimme a moment alone with his tubby ass, he's coming with me, and who knows, maybe a week with Fred or Wonkie, he'll lose a few pounds of flesh and come out with some coin and a whole new outlook on shit.

Maybe he'll come back week after week until ain't no weeks left.

Shit, no maybe about it.

Beats where he's headed now, some consulting gig in Orlando working for more pieces a shit like his friends here who are gonna be mean to him his whole life, pretend his wife and kids ain't fat as fuck too when he's around, or that him having a heart attack at thirty-five might surprise their sleazy company asses.

Much as my heart goes out to him, he's at least two-ninety, and no muscle up in there, which means he's slow and he sweats a whole bunch, a whole bunch too much when his knife flies out his hand 'cause his palms are all buttered-up.

Plus, biggums and his boys like to drink, no doubt, which means the shakes, which means I keep moving, son.

Shit, now this here's what I'm talking about.

Might just get home in time to tuck in my little Angel.

Track seven means I'm looking at some dude wearing a Baby Bjorn, walking in front of me with his wife who thinks she's kidding I don't know who with them Daisy Duke Dockers and that sleeveless thing.

She's pushing the stroller with the one-year-old boy

and pops can't stop looking at every lady who walks on by, don't matter whether she's fine, just anything better than what he's now realizing is the only piece of cold-ass box he's gonna be banging his whole life.

Ten times a year if he's lucky.

By appointment only.

He thinks mom don't see him looking, and even from back here, it don't take no Spinoza to tell she knows exactly what's on his mind.

Got his mall shirt tucked into his cargoes on a hotter-than-fuck summer day and can't keep his jaws from grinding he's so miserable.

Which means he's pulling in enough coin to feed them kids, get that house so moms can turn it into the Pottery Barn catalogue, and pay for the trip to Florida, which ain't no kind of vacation when all you're looking for is an exit.

He ain't getting paid enough that he's got that forever smile you get when you done crossed over.

He ain't never gonna neither 'cause he's always gonna be in the employ of the kind of player who did.

Moms just pointed at something to show his ass and he won't even look.

Yeah, this fool finna do anything to feed that hole.

He can't deal with there being a limit.

The eyes: they ain't the windows of nothing, they're the cameras of greed.

So what I know so far: One, he ain't gettin' no pussy, two, he hates himself 'cause it's all his fault, three he most definitely don't do drugs, and four he drinks sometimes, not enough to make me turn my head though.

With all that, you'd think I got myself a winner I could bag, tag and go on home.

Shit, you know what, the mom's just about as much of an easy win as her serial-killer-looking sorry excuse for a husband.

Only thing making her coming with me a little less likely is she's still breastfeeding.

Who knows, maybe we'll see each other again.

And there's only one reason why Bob, Bill, whatever his dumb ass name is ain't the one and it's on account there ain't no way he's gonna be able to get out of his old lady's sight for more than an hour.

Which is his fault, 'cause he – yup, there he goes again- can't stop looking at the ladies and licking his lips.

Wonder what he'd do if one of them bit. Whatever. Better you than me. Least my ass is in love.

I ain't trying to sound cold. Most folks just looking to get by and meeting me's same as the genie bottle rubbing up against them.

I mean how is what we do different from a boxing match? A football game? A stock car race? The stakes?

Least with us, it's straight up. You know what you're getting yourself into and ain't no one making you step in that living room, son.

Ain't no contract gonna make you step back in again either. You want out, you're free to go. It's the American dream. I hate violence. Hate it.

But we're helping people.

Looking for someone with that face tells me it's been over since a long time ago, like the dude I brought over last night: All Kindsa Crazy.

Someone by himself, who ain't no one gonna miss.

Someone with just enough of a violent past so when I tell him what it is, he ain't gonna swing on me.

Shit, how about someone who likes to get cut, who's looking for us, someone who found something on the internet and reached out.

Too hot for this shit anyway. Who's it's gonna be. You? No, 'cause track two means you're undercover. How about you?

Maybe if you wasn't walking around smiling like you was getting blown every second of your life.

Don't make me go into one of these bars neither looking for some broke-ass, divorced-as-fuck-and-just-gambled-my-daughter's-child-support- check-and-my-hooker-money sorry piece a shits. Don't make me go the easy route, son. Come and get you if there ain't no other way.

There's always another way.

Lopez, bossman, he told me once how you take ten random folks, tell them what the scoop is, easy paycheck, you just gotta stab a dude, that six of them finna think real hard and three to four's coming with you.

Now what the fuck's all this shit about?

Must be fifty cop cars and five ambulances in front of The Fountainhead Hotel.

All these dudes dressed in 1800's war clothes for some gay ass fake battle 'cause the fourth of July's tomorrow.

Damn, maybe some terrorist shit went down.

Ain't nobody look hurt though.

Except this dude in the back of the ambulance.

He's wearing an old school soldier uniform, got an icepack on his head, kind of looks like Andrew Jackson.

Mo'fucka look pissed too.

Cops are taking his statement about something and… nope, now they're yapping to some dude dressed as an Indian.

Shit, maybe this is a sign. Icepack's sitting there cussing to himself and everything. Maybe he needs someone to talk to. Ear. Shoulder if it comes to that.

Then we take a ride, find a way to relieve some of all that tension, talk about the future.

Which means here I come. Which means hello, how you doing? Which mean All Kindsa Crazy best get his ass back on an airplane.

9
LEG

How FRED MADE me steal the bus after he got plugged, ditch it in the Everglades, then douse the inside with kerosene and toss a match is all over the three o'clock breaking news in this tiny room on the twentieth-something floor of The Fountainhead Hotel in North Miami Beach.

I'm lying on the floor at the foot of the bed as the caffeinated voice above me says, "What's the matter, you get sick from being so high up? From the altitude? I used to get motion sickness like a cocksucker. In the car mostly. Which is weird, because I just read *In The Car* and drove three thousand miles out here from Boise without throwing up. Great book. Doesn't say too much about how to pay for gas and stuff. You should read it. It's about guys like us just a long time ago. They weren't into knives though."

Fred's on the bed getting some pink shit applied to where Arthur shot him by a stocky Iraqi person with a moustache who he introduced as Wreck.

Wreck's the surgeon the Beak pointed out last night.

He tells Wreck to teach Gretchen everything he knows about being a surgeon.

Wreck could be anywhere between thirty and sixty. Fred told me on the ride over here his surgeon is the closest thing he's ever had to a mother.

He stops applying the Calamine and glares at Fred, then stabs his arm with a syringe, busts out a square band-aid from his medical bag and slaps it over the larger bruise.

Gretchen's remained coiled at Fred's feet since Wreck made Fred sit and told him to take off his shirt.

Nobody's said anything about how Gretchen removed hers too.

"Want to know something weird about that book? The crazy guy, he's based on a real guy. That guy was cool as shit and died counting stop signs or something. He was forty-seven, which made me think, forty-seven years is the span of a working man's career, you know, eighteen-to-sixty-five, which made me think of the year 1865, and that's when they freed the slaves right, even though when you think about it, they kind of didn't."

Cic' would say, "Four out of five people are mentally disabled because they don't have the ability to clear their minds at will."

She'd say how theoretically we're all retarded, and not because we use such a low percentage of our brainpower, it's because we don't know how to stop thinking for two seconds.

"You sure you're not scared about all this? I'm scared some. A little bit. Not so scared I need to lie down with a knife in my hand and go to sleep or anything. Hey, maybe you shouldn't be doing this or you might pass out and get stabbed when it's your turn. Maybe you should go home before you get hurt."

What they're saying on the news is how a couple hundred yards back in the marsh, the body of a young man was found badly buried and recently deceased.

The shaky cam shows a snippet of a young man's leg sticking out of the swamp, a bloodstained sneaker attached to the foot.

Then they cut to the disturbed face of an Hispanic female anchor who says what a horrible thing this whole thing is and how she hopes they find Arthur, although they don't know who Arthur is and the police sketch they cut to is of some Arab-looking guy.

Now a brand-new high-top sneaker nudges me in the gut.

"Hey wake up, man, what do you think this is, a hotel?" Richie laughs.

Fred's gazing down at his bandages and saying, "Man's prepping for battle, Richie, can't you see this?"

"Dude, you got time, man, seriously. These guys will get us all straightened out."

Richie Green's the other me, the five-foot-two red haired seventeen- year-old with dozens of thin scars lining both forearms.

He arrived this morning and hasn't set foot in the living room yet.

He hasn't stopped talking since me and Fred got here a half an hour ago.

Fred said we should get to know each other and that Wonkie, the tall, tan and bald-headed person folding laundry on the balcony, has the pleasure of training Richie.

On the balcony, Alex, with a beard and scraggly hair in a ponytail, fires an air-pump BB gun at the tourists below.

He's wearing a *Bloody Stinkholes* T-shirt, the Brit-punk band from the eighties.

Beside him, Wonkie's a giant tattoo of zoo animals, portrait art of lions, bears, a few exotic birds, and one of a monkey on his ankle.

None of these guys have slept since leaving the living room last night.

And I guess the cops on TV are looking for me too because they superimpose a sketch beside the one of Arthur and say that anyone who has information about this angry Christian male should contact Metro PD detectives immediately.

The sketch of me is better than the one of Arthur, but not so good them finding me and convicting me of bus theft and arson is anything to worry about, especially considering my probable life span at the moment.

We all go out to the balcony and Wonkie hands me and Richie bundled-up rainbow-colored parachutes.

He points down at the beach, at a giant battlefield replete with mock forts, manned horses, fifty U.S. soldiers on one side, and fifty Indians on the other.

Alex fires a bunch of shots from his BB gun at a family of four, his veins bulging from his neck as he pumps and screams, "Pass the pork chops, dad!"

Fred says, "Need a little favor from you two," and puts another hand on Richie and tells us, "Every year since 1962 the Dade County Historical League stages a fourth of July celebratory war reenactment right here on the beach."

Fred leans against the balcony railing and tests its stability with a few nudges.

"This year it's Horseshoe Bend. Tennessee Infantry versus the Creek Indians."

"Let's go, show's about to begin," Wonkie throws in.

"You have to do something for me," Fred whispers, "you have to BASE jump into the crowd of tourists, team up with the Creeks and go get me Andrew Jackson's personally-engraved musket because it just happens to be the real thing. He's the General with the crazy white hair."

"This is how you repay me for Arthur," he says, "You score me that musket without getting picked up by the cops and we're going to be good friends. Best friends. Tom and Huck."

Alex coughs up a loogie and spits into the crowd below.

"There's one more thing," Fred tells me, "Because of our arrangement, you need to do this without letting go of your knife."

Richie laughs and Wonkie slaps him upside the head.

Wonkie explains the jump will be simple, that the trick is to get as much spring off the railing as possible.

He says if we hesitate even a half a second, we're ground burger, which, he says, makes this great practice for the living room.

Alex holds out a bundled-up rag and tells Richie to throw it on.

Richie folds out a wrinkled undershirt with an

ironed-on swastika and says, "That's not funny. My dad is Jewish. I am too sort of."

"Don't let him make you, Richie," Fred says, "With Alex, the joke really does explode in your face."

Alex stares at the ground.

Richie sighs at maximum volume and pulls Alex's gift down over his own shirt.

Wonkie straps the harness onto his chest.

"Richard," Fred smacks Richie on the back, "You'll fight alongside our troops. You'll fight honorably. I'm counting on you, son."

"Yeah yeah yeah, what can I even do for you today?" Richie's saying.

Fred pulls him close, "Wonkie and I have been friends a long time and although he may not be the type to come right out and say it, it is my opinion that although he may have grown up among considerable wealth and family devotion, there's always been something missing. What he needs is one of the feathers off the headdress of Chief Menawa."

"It's true, buddy. You'd be helping me fill the hole," Wonkie says.

"An orange one, right Wonkie?"

"Please."

"Man, you guys aren't my friends. You don't even like me. It's so obvious."

"'kay, up you go," Fred says as he and Wonkie boost him onto the railing where he wobbles a bit before falling ass-first onto Wonkie's outstretched palms.

"I'm not going to die am I?"

Wonkie buries the chute into his hand tighter, lifts him onto the railing and tells Richie to make a fist.

He says, "When I let go, you bend your knees and shoot out like an arrow. You've got this, little brother."

Fred tells him, "Meet us in an hour at The Scrambled Egg diner on Jefferson."

Richie takes a few breaths, asthma kicking in, just as we hear the call to battle below by way of the Army's bugle.

Fred says, "Remember, Chupa, green feather."

"Wait wait wait wait, you said orange! He said orange, Wonkie."

With what was intended to be a reassuring pat on the ass, Wonkie sends Richie plummeting toward the street as we all lean over, watching the rainbow chute blossom.

The landing isn't pretty. Richie manages to touch down in front of an oncoming Mayflower truck.

Richie rolls, tumbles, stands, runs, and rolls again, then rushes to the beach, and into battle in an attempt to join our troops.

I climb on the ledge.

"On the count of three," says Fred, "that's *on* three, Nipples."

"And let he who is not me perish in the bowels of Hades, tongue singed from the belly of the evil one. Amen."

Alex asks Fred what I'm quoting as I hold up my blade.

The three count is replaced by the ground rushing toward me at one hundred and twenty miles-per-hour.

10

JACKING ANDREW

THE TWENTIETH-SOMETHING FLOOR of The Fountainhead Hotel is not high enough for BASE jumping.

I manage not to land in the middle of oncoming cars, and slam into a crowd of tourists huddled around the perimeter of the beach.

The initial impact hurts wicked, and several are injured.

The pain recedes after a reasonable amount of applause.

I tear off my harness, hold my knife over my head and wail, "The hour of judgment is yourn and mine!"

Which earns me more applause, because everyone thinks this is all part of the reenactment.

In the fake beach battle there are far fewer Creeks than it seemed. Chief Menawa is easy to target because he's the only one in headdress.

To join them, I dart through the crowd and blaze into the sand, into battle, and into my destiny.

The bulk of the tribe are waiting behind the blockade and although the Americans have begun their charge, many a soldier has stopped in his tracks because of me, and Richie, who must be somewhere in the middle of Jackson's army.

I sprint toward the opposing armies, do a little serpentine footwork, and dive headfirst into battle just as the enemies collide.

I announce my arrival amidst gunfire pops and clanking swords with a healthy roar of "Repent!"

A giant black boot finds its way into my abdomen, then another, and for a second, the world turns white and silent.

In situations where hundreds of shiny leather boots and a few moccasins are stomping your belly to the rhythm of your screams, the thing to do is reach, grab, twist and pull, and I do, taking down some bespectacled infantryman nuts-first.

Back on my feet, I slap and threaten with the knife anyone who looks un-Indian and gets too close to me.

It's easy to tell the two sides apart, because the actors portraying the Creeks are covered with red makeup for authenticity.

Neither the Creeks nor the Americans understand what's happening.

These poor guys who volunteer annually to melt inside three layers of vinyl and bring joy to the crowds have now become the entertained.

I sound a war cry and charge an officer wearing a black codpiece thing around his neck.

When he shoves me, I use the momentum to jump

a few times and try and find Jackson as several rubber bayonets poke me in the side.

I push past a black medic, then charge some scrawny kid whose uniform is two sizes too big, who, on second look is a girl with short red hair like Richie's.

"Please," she's begging, frowning with a tilt of the head.

I take mercy and fell her with a head butt and cry out, "Riccchhhhiieee!" at the clouds in horror.

Richie emerges, floating in midair, surfing the hands of his own men, until a brawny militiaman holds him up with the ease of a paperweight, Richie pleading, "I give."

Too late though, because Richie's upside down as the soldier shakes him like a sack of dirty laundry.

I adapt to my newfound space. Soldiers and Creeks have stopped fighting.

Most of them are staring at me.

The loud painful thump is Richie hitting the ground, is the sound of my involuntary throat convulsion.

"Rejoice!" I scream, wielding my knife at the crowd.

A couple horses whinny and settle.

Up on the twentieth-something floor balcony of the Fountainhead Hotel, Fred and my other new friends are giving me their undivided.

Then, there he is, with the head of crazy white cowlicks, the rigid posture and those knife-edge cheekbones, propped up on a pale horse with a fancy military saddle and the whole regalia of official decorations: General's coat, a sword on one side and a shiny musket on the other.

I do not hesitate.

I begin my pissed-off charge, my face turning to

blood, eyes bulging to the size of ping-pong balls as I raise the knife and sack a terrified and tomato sauce-smelling Andrew Jackson to the dirt.

The crowd hugging the perimeter roars as I plant a sneaker into his balls, land on his gut with a flying elbow, and bite down on a white vinyl glove.

The hoots and hollers drown out his cries.

This beating, it's been a long time coming.

"Indians!" I yell, leap and land full force on his guts.

"Have," rinse and repeat.

"Feelings," and this time grind an elbow into his chest for Christ's sake.

"Too!"

Then for luck, I grab him by his lapels, prop him up and serve a family-sized portion slap across his tear-soaked face and notice the mixture of blood spittle, sand and white make-up coating my palm.

Jackson stares back at me with gray slits. Then he sees my knife wavering in the air.

"This is ridiculous," he says, a healthy strand of drool hanging.

"Tell your men," deep breath in, "Tell all your men, to push west."

"This is pretend," he spurts.

"West!" I scream and swipe the knife downward the way Fred taught me, intentionally missing.

"Push… Push west." his voice cracks.

"Command them, bitch! You want to live to see President?"

Taking a look around makes everyone start walking away from the Atlantic Ocean and toward California.

They might be walking toward the Gulf, but it's progress.

Some Creeks start to head off too.

"Not you Indians!" I have to yell at them, "This land is your land! You fuckers stay right where you are. You, Chief, pick up that dagger and bring it before me."

The Chief does as he is told, keeps his eyes locked on me at all times.

Underneath the red paint, the peacock on his head and the turquoise beaded shit across his chest, is a sad looking old Jewish guy.

The tourists and passerby watch, phones pointed at guess who.

The Chief says, "Kid, we can get you some help. There's still a chance for you."

But this is happening. And he knows it.

"You with the drum, start playing, nice and slow," I say. The Creek drummer taps to a very unsteady rhythm, which makes the crowd go nuts and start chanting.

As I circle Jackson, who revolves his neck to follow my gaze, I'm telling the Chief to turn around for a second, that he might not want to see this.

As the drum, the cheering and the chanting peaks, Richie rises up between two medicine-men, semi-conscious, and with my free hand I grab a chunk of wavy, spray-dyed white hair, pull it taut and with the other go to town with the knife in a sawing motion.

That none of Jackson's scalp comes off is relieving, as I extend my arm and display the prized lock up high.

The crowd goes apeshit.

I snatch Jackson's musket and sprint toward the street, where the tourists create an aisle of passage.

Random hands graze me as the aisle extends, blocking traffic, horns blaring, sirens screaming, me in fifth gear with my knife in one hand and Jackson's hair raised to the sky, singing at the top of my chords, "Repent!"

Over and over, "Repent now!"

11

SIMMER

To KILL SOME time before meeting up at The Scrambled Egg to hand over Jackson's musket, and also to avoid the cop cars and the helicopter, I visit a small church a few side streets away from the ocean.

Big surprise, it's empty.

The statue of Christ in the far corner recalls how I screamed at all those people on the bus earlier, and my conversation with Cicely.

I pull a few hairs from my head, then my chest, but it doesn't feel like anything anymore.

Just to show my disregard for his self-righteous poopy, I approach the statue and stab its face until paint chips fly in all directions and I'm yelling, "Bleed!" over and over until he's a caved-in rock of gray makeover.

As I catch my breath I notice the eye of a surveillance camera in the opposite corner zooming in on me.

I point my knife at the lens and the camera stares back with indifference as I rinse off with a couple splashes of Holy Water, then pee in the bronze bowl before heading back out to the street.

A method for blending when you're meters away from scores of cops who are looking for you, asking questions about you and are trained to find you, is to walk with chin high, proud and purposeful.

Make eye contact with as many as you can and shift your gaze before they look back at you.

As long as you're the first one to look and you don't look back a second time, no cop, medic, ambulance driver, Indian, or Infantryman will ever remember your face.

Neither will the Beak, who's chatting with Jackson at the rear of an ambulance.

No, they won't see you at all.

The nurse who stitched and counseled me after Coleman opened me up with his own blade six years ago taught me that.

The nurse who was a total stranger, and when she heard the details, everything that happened after the SUV crashed, couldn't look at me for days because, as she said, she could see my future.

The Scrambled Egg's got a neon plate of eggs, bacon and browns flashing on the sign out front, and is one of those late-night grease pits for the drunk and broken.

Wonkie, Alex, Bam Bam and Pebbles sit in a round booth with half- empty plates and glasses.

Pebbles smiles at me like I'm a six-week-old kitten. Her hair is flamingo pink.

Everyone in the diner murmurs about me carrying a knife and a musket, but when the manager approaches me with his palm extended I half-point toward the battlefield and he leaves me alone.

I take an end seat and wait for Bam Bam, Alex and Wonkie to pause in their conversation about homemade explosives to ask where Fred's at, then I see him sitting alone at a small table, staring out the window with a look like he just had his dog put down.

Bam-Bam puts Pebbles in one of those chokeholds that means he really loves her.

Pebbles asks me if I have a name.

Before I can answer, Bam-Bam's asking Alex if he can teach him how to make Nitroglycerin, his other arm flexing in a way that makes it look more muscular than it is, which is hard to do. His voice is tender.

Alex says "Nitric acid. Sawdust. Sulfuric. Ice cubes."

"How long did it take you to memorize that from Wikipedia?" Wonkie says as he swallows a fistful of fries.

"I could literally have you a back pack by five o'clock," Alex says.

Pebbles gives Bam-Bam an elbow to curb his interest.

Wonkie's saying, "One day soon this idiot's gonna walk into a crowded somewhere."

"Why would that make me an idiot?" Alex says. Alex looks exactly like Abe Lincoln, just shorter and with long hair. His eyes are all eroded from years of wearing contact lenses.

Pebbles sits up and punches Alex in the arm, which makes me laugh, but a second later she punches him in the side of the head, a real punch, and Alex shifts in his seat, avoiding her eyes.

She eases back into Bam-Bam's loving chokehold while Wonkie scans the placemat dessert menu.

Pebbles tells Alex to admit what he's hiding.

Alex stirs his ketchup with two fingers and says, "This one's up tonight," and he's pointing at me. "Same with Richie. Training's finished."

Excitement starts to make my guts glaze over and heal.

"I told you," Wonkie smirks and spits on the floor, "He's making a killing with those clips."

"You get paid every time, we all do," Alex says.

Wonkie says, "When I got here, this was straight up sports. Now he's turning us into fast food."

Alex keeps pointing at me, "This guy doesn't give a shit. Look at him."

"I'm not talking about that, talking about that kid getting killed in the living room, now he's throwing in this fool," meaning me, "and Richie, after what, a day?" Wonkie's saying, rubbing the lion tattoo on his arm.

When no one answers he glares at me. "So why the fuck are you here? You in debt? Or you just hate yourself and wanna die?"

"Why are you here?" I ask.

"I want to be a certified animal trainer. Have my own monkeys, panthers, parrots and shit. It's expensive, but I owe it to them. I owe it to the black rhino."

A hand grips my shoulder and squeezes.

Fred nudges in next to me and admires the musket.

"Where's Gretchen?"

"Organic Chemistry," Fred tells me.

He sighs and I notice two old ladies a table over staring.

"What?" I almost yell.

"What!" and do.

"You're an awfully disturbed young man," one of them says.

"Does your mother know how crazy you're acting?" the other one says.

"I'm not crazy," I yell, then realize I'm waving my knife.

Fred leans in, urges them closer with his finger and shakes his head when he says, "You ain't seen nothing yet," and for some reason this makes them melt into smiles.

Then he asks me if I require food, which gives me the melting feeling too.

"The Beak gave me some dough for you this morning."

I hold out my hand.

Fred's saying, "Yeah, we gave it to Arthur."

The old lady with the pearls at the table next to us is telling the other old lady to stop staring at Fred.

"You set all the money I have in the world on fire?"

"Arthur didn't want it, remember?"

"I'm so hungry right now."

He digs into his pocket, busts out a crumpled-up twenty, hands it over. "You go on and get anything you want, Nipples. My treat."

Wonkie nods toward the entrance where a battered Richie stumbles in, kicking the ground in self-pity.

And to say that when it rains it pours would be the Adolph Hitler of clichés, but some thick-chested, wide-eyed Jewish kid in a homemade T-shirt that says, "Cohen

Family Vegas Vacation!" looking sixteen tops, gets up from his table where his parents and younger sister eat fruit-filled crepes and pokes Richie in the chest, the poor kid having forgotten all about the not-so-nice symbol on his own T-shirt.

"Hey. Bud. What's up with that?"

Brother Cohen throws his arms up at Richie, who looks down, then counters with a dismissive, "Yeah yeah yeah, I'm Jewish," but can't finish the sentence, because the offended party drops him with the kind of punch that's so loud and hard you want to puke.

Wonkie takes a sip of water before heading over to Richie's rescue as a giant gleaming sneaker pumps its way into the guy's little ribcage.

Wonkie lifts Brother Cohen by a fistful of shirt and throws him a few feet as the mother screams and the father feels compelled to stand.

When Richie's attacker pops up and glares at us, this is when all the knives come out at once.

Not knowing the appropriate direction to point my knife, I halt the manager with the tip of my blade in his Adam's Apple.

Wonkie turns Richie over and the next gasp is everyone's.

"Ah, what the hell, man," Wonkie says, "Who's gonna fix this shit?"

Richie's jaw's popped out so far his mouth won't close.

He can't even cry right.

Everyone's eyes seem to find Alex, who barks at Little Sister Cohen when she grabs her mother's leg.

He screams at us, "He ain't even my trainee," while glaring at the whimpering child.

"You made him wear the shirt, limp-dick," Pebbles throws in, and Bam- Bam agrees by pouting his lips and nodding slowly.

Richie tries to say something, but it's just a prolonged vowel.

Alex says, "No way I'm doing it."

"Yeah, you are, you're doing it," Wonkie throws back.

"He's literally not my problem."

In the background, someone tells the manager to just give us the money while the restaurant version of *All Night Long* plays at an acceptable volume.

Fred steps forward and smiles an apology at the Cohen Clan, says, "You should do it, Wonkie."

"Call your new girlfriend, she's pre-med. Why I gotta do this?"

"Because, Richie likes you the best."

No one can argue with this.

A few diners run out the door, which means there's less than a minute until cops lose interest in their across-the-street investigation.

"Do it, brother, go ahead," Fred tells Wonkie again, and squats, giving Richie his hand to squeeze, smiling down on him.

I say two Our Fathers and one Good God as Wonkie sighs, holds Richie by both sides of his face and tells him to close his eyes.

Richie screams more effectively, which must be a good medical sign, even though his mouth still won't close.

Someone murmurs, "Looks like he really fixed it."

And the tension peters as much as tension can peter when five people are brandishing knives and one's holding a musket.

Brother Cohen calms his ready-to-lunge stance.

I place the knife down and take a sip of someone's tap water when Fred locks eyes with me.

He reaches into his waistline sheathe, saying, "Nipples? Why are you not holding what we agreed you were not to let go of?"

I gaze at my knife resting on the table before swallowing, then watch the Cohens and the whole restaurant hide under tables as Fred heaves his knife at me, and the others heave their knives at me, while I serpentine over and around people's tables and out of The Scrambled Egg unscathed.

From across the street, I watch patrons and staff streaming out and cops jogging over from the scene at the battlefield.

My new friends scatter in all directions, Richie dangling in Wonkie's arms, and Fred walking out with the musket, stopping to inspect it as cops run past him like he's not even there.

Like they don't see him at all.

Then I see my knife isn't the only thing that should have never left my hands.

In my mind, Fred unfolds a twenty-dollar bill, showing me Andrew Jackson's faded, crumpled, smarmy grin, then crumples the money into his fist.

12

THE KITCHEN

THE SPINE-WORN SELF-HELP manuals on the kitchen counter include, "Finding the Chill Zone," "When it's All on the Line," and my favorite, "For Crying Out Loud: A Ten-Step Guide to Calming the Inner You."

Part of me wants to open my mind and see if these car salesmen with online PhD's really do have all the answers.

How I got to the kitchen was Bam-Bam knocked on my motel room door tonight, took one look at me and said sit down.

He got me a warm rag, even held it to my forehead and told me in a calm voice about his first time, and how he stunk up the living room so bad everyone went into Lopez's back yard for fifteen minutes.

Bam-Bam said he stabbed a forty-year-old math professor who needed fast cash to pay a divorce lawyer in the stomach and didn't kill him.

He said he was aiming for his arm.

Bam-Bam said after his second meth bust last year,

his parents gave him rent and tuition money and said pick a city, just please go.

Pebbles, his girlfriend since junior high, joined him down here a few weeks ago and read about what Lopez does on some dark web forum.

Bam Bam doesn't want to hurt anyone, he does it for her, and Pebbles is starting to scare him.

He is studying Hotel Management at FIU. His real name is Brian O'Brian.

I've been standing alone in the kitchen for two hours. The kitchen sparkles. Stainless steel. No magnets on the fridge.

Some elevator version of a Brazilian song I can't remember the name of is supposed to be calming my nerves.

Comfort was here.

Soon it will be Richie leaning against the counter, and I'll be in the living room.

The self-help manuals mock me with their all-teeth gurus.

They're saying, "Fear is the bastard child of self-hatred."

They're telling me, "What you think are your real problems haven't even happened to you yet."

When the kitchen door swings open it's Fred wearing a black T-shirt with stab wound designs and blood dripping from every puncture.

"I'm scared, Nipples," he sighs, pressing index to forehead, rubbing in tiny circles.

Fred's saying, "I'm stopping this, companero. I can tell you want me to."

I shake my head.

I stop my foot from tapping on the tile.

I've put my hands in my pockets and taken them out five times since he came in.

"What happened to you that was so terrible you want to get stabbed and murdered so bad you can't stop jerking your arms around like a two-tentacled octopus?" Fred says.

Fred leans back, elbows on the stove, and stares at the ceiling. "Everyone's here for some fucked up reason. Everyone except me."

Fred's hand rests on my shoulder.

"I think you've been fiending for this since last night. Think someone took you to that place once and you liked it. And whatever he did to you, it's the reason you found us."

Fred tightens my fist around my knife and wraps each finger around the handle.

"Afterwards," I'm saying, my voice scratchy, "Go to my motel and find my phone. It'll ring within a few hours. Say something happened. Just make it hurt less."

"This person is the reason you won't kill yourself?"

"You can make it hurt less, right?"

"Yeah," he says, staring at the floor, "I can do that."

Moments later, I'm standing in the center of the living room.

The Beak and Kuba watch from the hall.

Fred, Wonkie and the rest of them sit on the floor and Lopez sets up his camera on the tripod.

Different color tracksuit this time.

The last thing Fred said to me in the kitchen was,

"Lopez wants to know if you're okay with this being filmed."

Which means this is the one everybody will remember me for.

"Look into the lens please," Lopez tells me.

After a second he thanks me, and with his remote control he turns up the soundtrack to that movie about the guy and the Indians.

13

KILLING PEOPLE

THERE'S A KNIFE in your hand.

You're standing on a plastic tarp between the TV and the people watching you.

Your palms might as well be covered in Crisco.

The sounds of your feet wrinkling plastic remind you of Christmas mornings before your mom disappeared and how you've never wrapped a present in your stupid life.

The door to the garage opens and a person walks in.

A man.

Older.

One of your ears starts ringing and you wonder if this noise is being created just for you.

This man standing a few feet away from you holding a medieval dagger has short-cropped black hair and he's tall.

He's wearing jeans with a long-sleeve flannel tucked in, a giant belt buckle, a wooden cross around his neck and boasts blade-sharp cheekbones.

That he doesn't seem surprised to see you means you

being in the living room is something he has been told to expect, maybe even promised.

Maybe Andrew Jackson was approached after yesterday's scalping, treated to a haircut and promised that if he agreed to step into this room without any sort of training, and do it on camera, that he wouldn't have to wait for what went around to come back, he'd be one of the lucky few who can serve their cold dish fresh from the plate.

Maybe he was told that as crazy as you might have seemed yesterday when you attacked his infantry, really, there was no way he couldn't win.

His eyes glean yellow and the glint runs circles on the tip of his knife.

Lopez turns up the music. He presses a button on the back of the camera.

Fred and Wonkie watch you with dead eyes from the floor.

Bam Bam and Pebbles are hugging so fiercely they're practically one person.

Alex's eyes say he wants to watch you bleed out.

The Beak's texting his wife while Kuba tries to nonchalantly read what he's typing.

The way you're seeing him now, he seems to be dressed as the real Andrew Jackson again, full regalia, General's coat and all.

After a blink and a half, he's back to normal, and his yellow eyes gaze back with the certainty that you don't even have the balls to stare back at him, and this is why you can't not lose.

This is the close-up you've been prepping for your

whole life, the opportunity that makes or breaks your career, for good.

You can feel Coleman buzzing around the room as the camera zooms in tight on your face.

Imagine an outside bar in the Florida Keys, steps from the bay, underneath a wicker hut, packed with tourists wearing visors and new T-shirts with the creases still showing.

Pretend there are six college kids at the bar, strung out from the road and stinky from the claustrophobia of the SUV they drove in all the way from West Virginia.

Then a stranger moseys over.

What if he was wearing his invisible wolf suit that night and moved smooth as a lens, zooming in behind them at the bar.

Maybe his name was Ronald Coleman and he had father's eyes and mounds of hair on his chest and neck, bunched in black sweat puddles under a button-down shirt with emblazoned swordfishes.

Could be this man claimed to be a retired real-estate lawyer who almost made judge, living on a boat off Elliot Key where he fishes as an excuse to not have to write, sometimes the reverse, chuckle chuckle.

What if he told this group of friends there hadn't been any drinking in nearly eight months, and he's got the yellow chip to prove it?

Cone stold sober, with an occasional shake of the fingers. Would anyone believe this made the papers six years ago?

"Action," Lopez is saying. "Someone begin, please."

You lock eyes with Jackson, who wears a frustrated

expression, nodding once like he really wants you to lift your shaking hand and bury the knife handle-deep into his chest.

Imagine a sophomore majoring in theater and his best friend Justin ate some little paper tab with a cartoon bunny etched in blue an hour before they stopped in Islamorada, a few minute's drive over the seven-mile-bridge, for a few hard-earned drinks.

Maybe this guy Justin started doing standing back flips, five years of gymnastics paying off as a favorite trick for dive bars and country bars and back home bars just like this.

What if the other five friends weren't laughing anymore because now they weren't alone?

Lopez says stop overthinking it.

The Beak says you need to quit hesitating and embrace shit.

Andrew Jackson purses his lips as your guts push toward your asshole.

Behind the sharp yellow eyes, you see a personal tragedy, which means maybe he's not stabbing you yet because he's here for the same reason you're here.

Let's say Justin was five-feet-two and tan, a wound-up pirate who compensated with arched eyebrows, a wicked cackle and bulging neck veins.

What made him stop mid-flip and notice the middle-aged bearded stranger?

One version might be when Cicely bit her lower lip.

Otherwise, Coleman might have blended right into the canvas, same as the set of shark's teeth on the wall of the bar: invisible when not examined with the relationship to its surroundings.

Lopez asks Andrew Jackson where'd all that bravado go.

Andrew's smile turns to dry ice.

The last few breaths before dying remind you of the feeling you get when the acid kicks in.

Starts in the hands, then moves its way up under your chin until all sense of weight is history.

You're losing pounds by the second, not including your cargoes and the rust-colored T-shirt your dead girlfriend bought you.

Form becomes as it is when seen through the right pair of glasses: empty.

Cic' would say this is you getting smarter.

Just fishing, but maybe Coleman's object was to become the secret love of all of them, make these college kids the first six wheels and him the axle, and sooner than later, to become the whole damned car.

If one were to take a stab at understanding the situation, maybe within the first minute Coleman knew they were on their way down to Key West, that the taller one with the hair of a horse was called Sy, was Justin's twin, a twin like Cicely, with the boy's haircut, the one with the thin lips she liked to chew, who was second's older than the gutless loser over yonder holding his girlfriend with the curly red ribbons for hair, both of them afraid to look too long at anyone.

You dodge left and crane your neck as the wind of Jackson's blade swipes inches from your cheek.

This is when the liquid warmth fills up inside your

boxers and blossoms over the scar on your thigh. Now you're both moving around the room.

Consider this goofball actor knew when Coleman asked Cicely and Elizabeth what college they went to, and the words rolled out of his throat cowboy-slow, and Elizabeth answered him all cutey-pie, that he must have known she was pasty-faced from the humidity, was addicted to hair-pulling, costumed herself in tie-dye rags, and wrecked two Porsches on ecstasy before she turned eighteen.

This pussy-whipped reject might have thought by the way the sea cowboy's fingers couldn't stop shredding the napkin wrapped around his glass of lemonade that to Coleman, the presence of three young guys made no difference.

Pretend for a moment his sister saw him see these things, because he and Cicely shared perceptions.

Could be Cicely never said a word because her fragile bones couldn't take any more jabs of people calling her crazy.

This puny douchebag's clearly confused girlfriend Betsy might have clasped his thigh when she felt it shaking.

She might have been just a sweet girl from Queens who understood and accepted his smelly-ass, figured paranoid and obsessive was better than jealous and possessive.

It's a safe bet this cowardly idiot in question pulled the only girl who'd ever thrown him a bone a little closer, a year of fawning her from a distance to catch up with, pulling her by her pot-belly and squeezing into her as two bar stools away, Elizabeth twisted a braid around her finger, yanked, and the sea cowboy produced an egg.

A simple egg.

No cracks.

Squeezed in the palm of Coleman's hand and they're all three crowded around save the lovebirds and the sister, giving nature a college try, squeezing the perfect structure and it never breaks, and Justin, acid-eyes wide and juicy, couldn't believe the miracles of science.

When Cicely went to the car and lay in the back seat, Ronald Coleman, who told us his name was Barry, called this the closing arguments.

As your face smashes into the bookshelf and small chunks of gnarled flesh and blood slide down the surface of Andrew Jackson's blade, it sinks in what Fred meant by being one with the knife.

You might have thought of this a second ago, before the blood crept into your eyes and your ear went numb, right about the time you dropped your knife and saw your thin reflection glaring back at you.

Then it would be Jackson with his ear hanging on his shoulder by a few gore strings.

You hear Lopez telling Andrew it's not over until there's penetration and you drop your knife again.

There were two sets of twins: Justin and Sy, Cicely and Gabriel, and the remaining girls, Betsy and Elizabeth, who'd been joined at the hip since freshman year.

Elizabeth offered Coleman this information. So he offered a boat ride. Just for kicks. Said they'd make Key West in two hours. Said this would be his pleasure.

Staring into his glass at a wavy funhouse reflection,

downing the lemonade, and rubbing perspiration on the side of his faded britches was Coleman's final call to action.

Your ear's on the floor now and isn't really an ear anymore.

On the way to Sy's SUV, Coleman told Elizabeth he wore a wedding ring for hope of reconciliation, said he was in the middle of a divorce, partially the reason behind the retreat down south, away from the lawyering gig in Fort. Lauderdale.

He crawled in the back, left window, next to Mr. Brilliant Actor, who asked where do you come from, Barry, and how did you get to the bar in the first place.

Then Coleman was the one who wouldn't lock eyes, said "No further questions," before he licked his lips and teeth.

Andrew Jackson isn't trying to stab you anymore and no one's moving.

Andrew's telling you to do it so he doesn't have to slice you up again.

The acid was in overdrive and Justin squeezed the egg in the front seat until his jugular moved around, a snake with its head cut off, and every time all of his strength couldn't break the egg, he whispered in hushed surprise, "I fucking love you people."

Andrew Jackson's saying don't look at me, just put it in.

He's saying it like everyone else can't hear him even though they still have all their ears.

It's been said they were squeezed in back, Sy speeding

down Highway 1, listening for Coleman to tell him the turnoff.

Sy wanted to be a Taoist, enjoyed breath work and prided himself on never raising his voice like his brother Justin.

Elizabeth, sitting on the center console, certainly put on the *Inflatable Jockstrap* CD and Betsy first thought the heavy breathing sounds were the music, and not her miserly excuse for a boyfriend.

She must have been thinking she was too heavy for his lap.

In the blink of an edit, Jackson moves the blade along his neck and isn't pressing very hard.

Then the dripping on the tarp, faster as he falls into a lump.

You're cradling the man in your arms, not because you forgive him for all the bad things he's done to the Indians, or spreading your ear and your blood all over the room, it's just that this isn't the first time you've watched someone's soul drain from their irises and for the life of you, you can't figure out why this is making you cry.

Lopez is saying they need to clear the room and set up for the next thing.

When all you do is hug Jackson tighter and then try to give him mouth to mouth until you're tasting blood and meatball sauce, that's when what's left of your ear begins to sizzle, a thousand needles stabbing and you close your eyes migraine-tight in an attempt to make it stop.

Without a doubt, he said, "Turn right" two times before Sy heard him.

The music was messing up his mind and Coleman

used the momentum of the turn to lean forward and reconfigure the layout of everyone, saw Cicely faking sleep with her head on the window, her exposed neck longer than he realized.

Kuba and The Beak have to pry the dead old suicidal bastard off your lap as Lopez takes the memory card out of his camera and heads toward the kitchen, beckoning you out of the living room with a sheepish smile and words you're glad you can't hear.

Something guttural filled the SUV as Sy sped down the back road. Justin couldn't stop laughing and the high beams revealed a yellow dead-end sign up ahead, in front of a silver barricade and Elizabeth turned down the music.

This was when they all heard it, smelt the salt, and according to reliable sources, before our little hero could touch his girlfriend's heart, he felt Coleman's first move, rolled over on her, never seeing the knife that slid into his thigh with a melon crunch.

14

BIRDS

"SAFETY IS OUR first priority," Lopez told me a week ago after the fight as I bled in his kitchen.

Wreck the world class surgeon cleaned and stitched and bandaged me while Fred whispered over one of my shoulders that Richie's up next and if anything like what just happened to me happens to Richie, he'll never see any of us again and we'll go to the cops.

Fred whispered this to Lopez, behind my other shoulder as Lopez laughed a little and repeated, "Safety, young man, is our first priority."

The priority didn't end up applying to Richie though, who The Handle carved so perfectly across the belly he barely spilled a drop.

The Handle wiped his shiny gray blade on Richie's jeans.

The three-piece-suit, the wired specs, the briefcase and the one glass eye that glares at you no matter where you are in the room, all of it scares me.

Fred told me The Handle is not The Handle's real name. He said The Handle is a residential realtor, and not a successful one. He put his blade in his briefcase and left the six of us anesthetized. Except Wonkie.

Wonkie's veins popped out of his arms when The Handle walked into the living room and casually slit Richie, before the hush of disbelief passed.

What tore Wonkie up the most was Richie went out thinking he'd been betrayed by the one guy who actually liked him.

Even The Beak came over to where we all sat and whispered in my ear how somebody fucked up, that he didn't want me to get the wrong idea about Lopez and what we did in the living room, but with the remainder of my left ear bandaged, I wasn't hearing any of it.

Besides, the giant TV screen kept looping my ear getting hacked off in slow motion.

My breakthrough performance.

My retirement party.

Then the Beak and Kuba carried off dead Richie with stuff spilling out of him and Fred stepped onto the tarp, twirling his blade.

A second later a lanky man wearing a faded Alligator shirt joined him.

Lopez saying go and Fred raising his arms, tightening his gut.

The Alligator Shirt's knife entered halfway, silent, painless.

Pebbles told me Fred had done that before, let himself get stabbed so the other person could take the money and go solve their problems.

This time wasn't like that though.

Fred's expression in the driveway of Lopez's house, reclined in the front seat of Wonkie's Cadillac as Wreck sewed him up with fierce intensity couldn't have been any different if one of us had suggested going out for some late-night donuts.

Wreck insisted on giving his patient some Demerol, or an exotic Morphine cocktail.

Fred laughed, flipping through radio stations and before my thought made its way into a question, he replied, "Nipples, are you even aware that Lopez tried to kill you tonight?"

The Beak knocked on my motel room door a few days after my opening night, sat me down and explained how it's been decided that my services are no longer needed in a way that would require me to use a knife.

That they would like to keep me on as a consultant, which means training people, which means they're sure anyone who studies under me will walk into certain death, paint blood for the camera in exciting and original ways, and keep Lopez supplied with content.

This is why Fred, Wonkie, and Bam-Bam gave their unwritten resignations.

Everyone except Alex and Pebbles.

It's why Bam-Bam got in his Trans Am and went home.

The roof of the donut shop overlooks a Chinese restaurant. Pebbles chain-smokes cloves, let's the ash run with gravity. Tonight's been wet and windy, the occasional cat scurrying into traffic, some of them lucky.

Pebbles asks me to stop flexing my bicep and staring

at it like I think she can't see me doing it, and without pause, asks where I'm taking Scar, the new person, to get him ready for his big day tomorrow.

Pebbles' real name is Jacqueline.

She told me this.

She told me she's addicted to stealing from drug-stores, and has always wanted to live in Corpus Christi, even though she's never been.

It's just the sound of the name rolling off her tongue that speaks to her.

She told me all of this because she was grieving, and still is.

A Gallinazo vulture flies by and reminds me of Comfort.

Pebbles started coming up here at night after Bam-Bam went home to Philly.

She flicks her clove into the wind, shivers and wraps her arms around her chest, which she could feasibly accomplish twice at her size.

When I pull her close, she allows her trembling body to fall into the crook of my arm.

"Some of us are just meant to get stabbed to death," she tells me.

Another vulture flies by.

15

SIX DUDES

THE QUARTER-SHAPED WOUND I can't stop imagining is on the back of my head becomes sensitive every time Scar spits, his thick skull butting toward the ground of the alley, almost in protest.

He does this when he's supposed to be listening.

It's his funeral, but making sure this short, stocky pit bull walks out of the living room tonight is what they're paying me to do, or not do.

Because everyone says things have changed since I got here.

There is no longer a training period.

Now there is only a brief conference with people like me before new players get to it.

Players like Scar, with hairy Popeye arms, shorts that come down to his calves, and blue ink creeping up from under his collar.

"What, uhh," he half points, then grabs his lobe, "Happened to your ear, man?"

"What ear?"

"Yeah, right."

"Let's stop talking."

We're standing in an alley between a jewelry store and a shop that sells ten-dollar T-shirts with funny sayings. *Miami is for Me* or *I am a Graduate of Beer University.*

No puddles in this alley.

No cats, bums, crack vials, graffiti or broken beer bottles.

The dumpster smells fine.

While the Everglades might be the perfect place to prepare Scar for his debut, it's not all that necessary, because he'll manage, or he won't.

"Give me your knife."

He removes a camouflage hunting knife from his waistline.

"We don't have much time. So do me a favor. Check out that decrepit five-story building across the street. Look real hard, tell me what you think you see."

"Tell me, man. Bust out the preach. Wait, let me guess, it's not just a place some poor folks live. Right?"

From a distance, this apartment building appears unquestionably whole, yet chances are few of the residents inside know one another beyond the obligatory nod.

But from here people watch all these lives in windows as they appear so perfectly unified, a family of healthy white blood cells swimming in a stream.

"You know you're scaring me, right? Why are you making me peep buildings and looking at me all bug-eyed and not saying shit? This ain't a cult, is it?"

Scar pretends to shiver.

"Why did you come here?"

"Some dude called The Beak said he could get me a grand for a few minutes work. No gay shit he told me."

"Why do you need the money?"

"Just want to get paid, buy some new clothes, pay my rent."

"What's the percentage of your brain that you use?"

"Brain percentage, what, they say we don't use all we could."

"We average four percent. Six and you're a genius, able to slow down your heart rate at will, beginning to understand your central nervous system."

"Cool. Now, give me back my knife. Please? Nipples, right? Take your hands off me, man!"

"At ten percent you'll have a photographic memory and the CIA will start sending you emails. At twenty you'll have the gift of Telekinesis and suspended animation, like grizzly bears, you'll be able to go without food and digestion for up to six months sans the loss of any significant weight."

"Sans?"

"Thirty: the gift of flight, multiple orgasms, clairvoyance and mind control. Forty: you can kill people with a snap of the fingers, set armies in motion with a thought, drain the Atlantic or bring down jumbo jets. Fifty and you'll no longer require the use of your body."

"Bro. Seriously. If I ask you again to keep your hands off me, I'm going to injure you. Sans the knife."

"Sixty and you've transcended thought and sound, in the realm of the lesser Gods. Seventy and you are God. You're the planets, stars and gatekeeper of black holes.

Eighty and you revolve around time, you are eternity, a personal scrapbook of infinity, beyond God because you're very essence created the universe. Ninety percent and galaxies are cells within your fingertip, if you had a fingertip, which how could you when even the word gas would be too solid of a term. When you reach ninety-nine percent, it's time to sit back and chill, swim back and forth through time at will, create a planet, destroy one, because one more step up means it all ends for good, blackness, if there was still such a thing."

Scar wraps three fingers around my wrists and pushes my hands from his neck.

Palm up, what he's saying is he understands the implications of emptiness versus form, that once the knife finds its way into his hand, the only successful way of using it will be to embrace our discussion.

One last chance. In one hand, his knife, in the other, the fifty bucks Lopez gave me to train him.

"What, you're paying me now? For what?"

"Pick one. You take the money, you walk away, go to the mall, go home. You want, come back in a month, you'll get twice the amount, all for allowing me to save your life."

Scar takes the money.

He also grabs the knife, points it at my face, and laughs to himself.

"Killed six dudes last year. Right now, I could beat you to death with my bare fists and who's gonna come after me? You want to save someone, you walk. Naw. You know what? You stay right here. Three percent of my brain and proud of it, bitch. Today you're the one's getting saved. Weird-ass mother fucker."

With one last loogie from the pit of his guts, Scar christens my sneaker and moves out of the alley pocketing my personal training fee.

The invisible wound on the back of my head itches and flakes to the point that scratching it makes my fingernails fill with blood.

16
BUSINESS LUNCH

She's saying, "We watched the video where he lost the ear. We think we can do business."

She takes a bite of her salami sandwich and wipes her mouth as she chews.

"My associate is worth well over two hundred million dollars. He's a silent partner in one of the most lucrative car wash businesses in Western Europe. He owns several restaurants and sits on the board of over ten corporations."

Gayle Shapiro's associate wants to buy the videos of what we do in the living room.

It's why Lopez, me and The Beak are having lunch at a small outdoor table at some Coral Gables deli.

Why I'm here is still a mystery.

Gayle clears her throat, dips into her attaché and produces a leather- bound proposal, which she passes around to everyone except yours truly.

The Beak scoots closer and places the binder between us. Gayle folds both hands under her chin and leans forward. "The way we see the online release, it will be your introduction to the world, your coming-out party if you will, a chance to say hello in a way that's not walking into a conversation, waving your arms around and screaming at the top of your lungs that you're here and you're staying. It's all a part of the process."

When Gayle says "process," she accentuates the "o."

Lopez flips through the proposal three times while sucking down a corned beef bagel, spits out some lettuce when he asks, "What does this mean: *Ancillary Prospectus' Simplified Overview and Analysis of Open Market?*"

"Maybe I don't have your education," Lopez slurps and swallows, "but I don't think what's in that folder means anything at all."

"Word, man," The Beak throws in, placing a hand on my knee and squeezing.

The Beak whispers, "Why you keep scratching the back of your head, dog?"

"Let me simplify, because that's really what I'm here to do," Gayle says.

Gayle says, "My associate is clear on one thing: What you," and she points a crooked, yet well-manicured finger at all three of us, "what all of you are doing is so the next logical step in reality television."

The lines around Lopez's mouth form two wrinkles as The Beak laughs out of his nose.

"And that's just the beginning, yeah, it is. After a year, two, we expand to pay-per-view, novelizations, film-franchises and beyond. Imagine a Richie action figure with retractable intestines. This is what the people want. Not to watch people die for the thrill of it, no, what they want, what is important to audiences worldwide, it's caring about the characters before they die. And it can all be propelled by the question: Is? This? For? Real?"

A table full of silence means the noise in our heads is deafening.

The Beak signals a time-out, laughs his way into leaning forward, "Hold up. All right. What I'm hearing, and if I'm wrong I'll shut the fuck up, is you want to go full spread with everything. You understand, I hope, that we figured you wanted to buy these videos and shit and sell it off underground, you know, to rich folks in weird ass countries who for them ain't nothing ever gonna be enough."

Lopez furrows one of his chins and looks to Gayle for a reply.

"Well," she says, "we're a little more optimistic about it. Look, sugar, the average viewer wants to see a combination of conflict, competition, reality, suffering and triumph. Other people's weakness uplifts us all whether we care to admit it."

The Beak's leaning closer, ready to jump over the table, "You hear a word I said? Last time I checked, stabbing folks was a felony."

Gayle waves her arms in defense, "Legally, everything's up for grabs anyway. You read the news. Money doesn't make laws. Money is the law. So long as all the right people get their tributes in a timely manner, by the time whatever renegade lawyer was successful in court, we'd have made all of this the norm by contemporary community standards. Through an eensy-teensy amount of violence, we can help make a better world."

"You're talking like a crazy person," Lopez tells her. "What's the offer?"

"Fifteen hundred per video. Three thousand if someone dies."

Every time Gayle completes a sentence, she emits a potato-salad-burp stench.

Chunks of silence fill the sticky air as tiny white planets dance around Lopez's tomato-colored head.

"Sounds about right," Lopez says.

"If you make a movie, who's gonna play me?" The Beak says, arms folded high on his chest.

Gayle smiles, "In terms of fictional material, you might not factor in, sugar."

"You best re-factor, stank! Who you think makes shit happen up in this bitch?"

"One more thing," Gayle says. "We want more videos with the guy who lets other people stab him."

Lopez's lower lip flattens. "Fred is no longer with us, unfortunately."

"It's a shame," Gayle says to the table, "The camera really likes him."

"We can find others who will do what Fred does," Lopez says.

"Really likes him," says Gayle. "What needs to happen to get him back in the living room?"

Now everyone's staring at me, and why Lopez asked me to meet them starts making serious cents.

17

DARLA

IT'S JUST ME at the dresser mirror in my motel room shirtless, wearing my tighty-whities, and flexing my doughy abs.

The long scars on my chest and sides from Coleman's blade have stretched with age. Right now, I'm holding the phone to the ear that Andrew Jackson didn't chop off before offing himself.

The automated woman's voice on the phone is saying:

Using your touch-tone keypad, please describe the type of girl you would like to speak with.

After my midnight scavenge for the street sweeper, I found two brochures advertising free phone sex.

For Asian, press one. For African-American, press two. For Middle-Eastern, press three. For all other options, please press the pound sign. Thank you. For fetishes, press one now. For bondage, press two.

For incest, press three.

For bestiality, strangulation, Greek, snuff, orgies, and gangbangs, please press the pound sign.

I want the girl I choose to sound like Comfort.

What she'd sound like if she'd ever made a sound around me.

I press whatever button matches her in no way at all.

Please listen carefully, as our options have changed.

For hand relief, press one.

For instant penetration, press two.

For safe sex, press three.

For oral, anal, and BDSM, please press the pound sign.

I take a seat at the foot of the bed and fall back.

One hand down my tighty-whities and the other scratching the back of my head until my nails are sticky.

Thank you.

One moment please.

The on-hold jingle sounds like a cockroach's thoughts before being crushed by an empty ketchup bottle.

What if the wound on the back of my head is Psoriasis.

Forget hair pulling and Jesus, what if what's really wrong with me will mean pretty soon I can't wear dark shirts anymore.

But then what if the Psoriasis gets so bad, instead of wearing white shirts to hide the flaking, I wear all black, just to feel like everybody else?

Thank you.

You are now on with Darla.

When the automated voice says the name of the girl, it's a recording of another girl's voice.

Darla's voice.

Darla says, *So you want to play rough, big guy? Why*

don't you get on your hands and knees. That's nice, baby. That's nice.

Now, tell mama what you want me to do.

Every time I hear a girl's voice, I wonder if this is what my girlfriend might sound like now if she'd continued to age.

Maybe Darla is really Comfort.

What if after she stabbed William, she hauled ass out to a strip mall near the airport, found the same sex pamphlet as me and decided upon a more anonymous mode of employment that still managed to give her an outlet for her dusky nature.

Or maybe she did this before she even stepped into the living room.

Maybe this recording is six years old.

The previous woman's voice comes back on and says, *If you would like Darla to spank you, please press one.*

For whips and chains, press two. To have Darla stick two fingers up your… I'm sliding my hot nasty fingers all the way in, baby. You like that? I knew you would. My pussy is soooo wet. Uh huh. You want it deeper? There we go? How about one more finger?

For another finger, press one.

For four fingers, press two, for fisting, please press three now.

Cic' would say the truth is found by analyzing more carefully to discover what will really make one happy.

Yeah, baby, yeah, spread that cornhole for mama. Let's spread it all the way.

What Darla's saying makes me think of a grilled cheese sandwich, which makes me kind of hungry, but food thoughts come with horrible images, such as eating a pizza while watching the autopsy channel.

Right now, two fingers can't even jumpstart this disaster. The only turn-on is having to choose. *Are you ready to fuck me now, baby? Or do you want me to read you a story first?*

If you would like to have sexual intercourse with Darla, please press one now.

For deep-throat oral, press two, for anal, press three.

If you believe you are going to cum, please press the pound sign.

Something about the operator makes the experience more uplifting.

Having to make choices means making the wrong choices, but why that's arousing me I have no idea.

For facials, press one. To ejaculate on Darla's breasts, please press two. For sfelching, press three. For snowballing, press four, or press the pound sign for more options. I'm sorry, but you have pressed an incorrect option. For facials… I'm sorry, but you have pressed an incorrect option. For facials… I'm sorry…

18

MUTATIONS

Recycling. In one sense, everyone's making their contribution. Like they say, "It's a start, right?" It is a start.

These days if a person puts an empty plastic water bottle in gen-pop trash, not only could he face a fine in many states, but his neighbors won't like him.

Dirty scowls.

Cold shoulders.

For sure, no freshly baked Zucchini bread come late November.

Plastic belongs in the bin with other plastics, aluminum cans, and glassware.

In the other bin goes disregarded paper products, empty egg cartons, sex pamphlets, or shredded phone books.

What's funny is ecologically-aware neighbors take great pains to get throwing stuff away just right, then pile all four kids into their monster trucks so they can enjoy being at eye level when they get to the drive-thru window.

"Are you going to slap someone again, Nipples? You have that look like you're gonna slap people."

Right now we're in Coconut Grove, at the office of Dr. Leonard Sherman, F.A.C.S, the only plastic surgeon in the area who would see us.

We're not seeking plastic surgery because there is anything we want fixed.

This is about something nobler.

Something to inform the world and ourselves all about how to look inward, so what's deep down shines through on the surface.

"So. Boys," the doc says, sitting down at the little desk in his office, "Gotta tell you, you're lucky you got me. January's a busy time. Lots of folks looking to make a change."

Sherman takes a bite out of a peach and squirts juice on his trifocals, then doesn't bother to clean off.

He says, "You two have something particular in mind?"

From the other side of Sherman's desk, Fred and I watch the juice run down his lens.

Fred fields it. "Doc, I think I speak for both me and my associate when I tell you we have a lot of things bothering us."

"Do tell," he says, slurping the peach, "'cause from where I'm sitting, I see two good-looking young guys, minus your friend's ear debacle. Otherwise, I'm guessing these image-related quirks lie beneath the surface. Dare I say: mutations?" He holds out both hands in mock defense.

Leaning forward in his chair, Fred says, "Doc. Your milk is homogenized by default."

"Not sure I follow."

"You got mutations for us, we'll take 'em. How much for the worst mutation?"

"Are we talking penile enlargements? Implants? You heard of the pump?"

"Pump isn't gonna cut it. Well, I can't speak for my dark side over there, but… what I mean to say is, what bothers us the most, stems from inside, and why we're here is to see if you can use all of your skills to make the inner us's agree with the outer I's."

"Sure," he licks his fingers, "That's the basis of all plastic surgery. People want to look and feel their best. Sometimes, a little tweaking on the outside can do wonders for self-esteem."

"See, that's the problem," Fred smiles, removes his knife from his pocket and waves it in the air, "We have too much self-esteem. Us not having any complaints is our complaint. What we need is a classic case of Gynecomastia."

"You want me to give you breasts? Can do."

"Maybe on one side, and minus the nipple. How about some wrinkles? Or facial scarring. What would be your fee to, say, give my friend here Hypohidrotic Ectodermal Dysplasia? You know, the thing that prevents formation of hair, fingernails, teeth and sweat glands? The kind of thing that allows a male pig eight-minute orgasms. Ooh, can you give us that?"

The Doc spits the peach pit at the trash and misses.

I crawl over and place it where it belongs, then return to my chair.

"You think that knife means you have self-esteem? Young man, I've done more brilliant things with a knife than you can fathom."

Fred raises his knife and stabs Sherman's tie through the desk.

After he retracts it and puts the knife back in his pocket, he apologizes.

The Doc is on his feet, finger inching toward his phone.

"Have a seat, Lenny, and let me try and be more specific. I really do insist."

Sherman's arms shake when he lowers himself back into the leather chair.

Fred clasps his hands behind his head before explaining, "You offer doses of perfection. We believe there's no such thing, yet at the same time, the rest of the world strives for this. So, what we propose, is if you can damage us ever so slightly, to make us more natural, not only would you be helping us make our statement, kind of uncommodifying us, but in turn, you could bring our inflated egos back down to Earth so that we don't have to live as overdogs, and resort to deadly knife-play in the offices of cross-dressers."

Sherman gazes around himself to see what gave him away.

"Overdogs. Sure," Sherman says, "Get the fuck out of my office. My brother-in-law's a cop, you know?"

"Then you won't help us?"

"Son, my time is extremely valuable."

"Then why didn't you say something," Fred says, reaching under his shirt for a rubber-banded wad of hundreds, funded by almost thirty stab wounds. Blood money. Sherman's eyes perk.

He flips through it and hands it back. "'kay. Call me re-interested."

"Let's say we wanted a few inches added to our noses, plus maybe one of those crooked bone things up top," he points to Sherman's nose, "the Jewish thing, what are we talking about."

His chin sunk in a hopeless palm, Sherman explains, "That's not possible."

"Could you make his other ear stick out more?" meaning me, "It's always bothered him."

"Sure. That's easy," Sherman says, "What else?"

What happens next is Sherman takes some Polaroids of us and says he'll run a few possibilities on the computer.

When we're alone, sitting next to each other Fred says, "The soles of your shoes are on their last glue string."

I stare at my sneakers.

"Here," he says, removing a hundred from his wad, "Buy some shoes. And a toothbrush."

"I have a toothbrush."

A few chunks of silence before Fred says, "That's really gross."

"What?"

"You're scratching the scar under your shorts, then sniffing your fingers and looking at me to make sure I don't see you. I do though. It's pretty nasty. You do a lot of gross things."

"Like what?"

"Like pulling hairs out of your head and beard all the time. Breathing too close to people. What else, uhh, you smell like a boloney sandwich. Your mouth never closes. Next to the scar picking and your manicotti ear, the wiping the sleep from your eyes and eating it thing takes first prize in the disgusting category you seem to have conquered."

"You even like me at all?"

"You know you're my favorite, Nipples."

A few minutes pass, then I ask, "Like me better than Wonkie?"

"I've known Joaquin since first grade."

"Alex?"

"Hands down."

We walk out of there an hour later with computer-generated images of what Fred referred to as the future us's.

At the bus stop he whispers in my good ear, "I mean, why else would I hang out with you every day? But quit the best friend shit. You should know better."

His scan still makes him more handsome than me.

"What would have been ideal is if Lenny could suck all the fat out of my lips and stuff it in my cheeks. You have to admit the arched eyebrows will make me look more menacing."

He says, "You think Gretchen will still love me with an elongated chin?"

My scan reveals what might be a revolution in the field of cosmetics.

We decided the removal of my nose was the first ideal

step, sort of Pinocchio in reverse, the idea being to make me less of a real boy, plus a permanent curl of the lip as a way of exclaiming my dissatisfaction not only with myself, but the world around me.

Lastly, and this is key to the entire procedure—Fred's idea also—we've opted for widening both my eyes to full distension to create the illusion of perpetual surprise.

The doc tried to insist he could do wonders for my ear, but my personal trainer told him unless he could mangle the other one just as perfect, we had no business rocking the ugly boat.

"I don't have any money to pay for this surgery," I say.

"Don't worry, Nipples, one way or another we'll find a way to destroy ourselves."

19

THE JESUS EXTREME

THEY'VE GOT ME all wrong.

It's been that way since the beginning and the beginning was not a year-and-a-half ago at James Madison University when Wonkie forwarded me an email from beak@knifepeople.org that he'd received a few days before, offering him paid airfare and motel in Miami, and asked me what my plans were next weekend.

It was him they wanted, because of the man's reputed violent streak, and his affiliation with the extremest of sports in a solo capacity.

Wonkie's the guy who base jumps from skyscrapers before the brink of dawn, dives through the crack in the ice for an afternoon swim, and knocks off Federal banks in Wisconsin while on his way to the Boise Circus to free the elephants.

He even makes it into the vault, keeps a hundred thousand and sends the leftover cash to the Association for the Emancipation of Koalas.

That's why he got the email.

They never wanted me to begin with.

The beginning wasn't even my last year at the orphanage in Clark County, Indiana, or that day when the Applebaums, my third set of foster parents, used me as farm labor, tanning belt beatings and everything, but didn't expect a surprise visit from Colonel Francis, the orphanage director, who punched both Applebaums to death right there in the wheat field and then told me in between breaths and bloody palm wipes that he'd never lost an orphan yet.

The Colonel had an obsession with saving kids, still does today, and telling him that the Applebaums' beatings hadn't caused me a shred of pain would have been impolite.

That was on my twelfth birthday.

Again, not the beginning.

If they didn't have me all wrong, people would know Fred Reynolds hasn't experienced the sensation of pain since he was six years old and his father came home from the office, sat down to dinner, and when Fred's mother asked about her husband's day, shot her in the nose, then shot Fred in the stomach, along with his two older brothers, even shot the Chocolate Lab, then picked at his mashed potatoes before placing the sixth bullet in the side of his brain.

Since then, pain feels like the most selfish thing in the world. Nobody has the right, especially when you've seen what's out there. That was the beginning. They've got me all wrong.

Because when Lopez asked me and Wonkie a year ago

in his kitchen if we would be interested in giving this a go, I knew the people agreeing to do this to themselves might need some kindness, and if letting them keep their lives, make a few dollars, and feed their children means a few little knife scars, then what's there to think about?

Why not focus my thoughts on something other than me?

If you can do that, then a knife going through you won't have a sensation, so long as you are one hundred percent focused on something else.

Violence shocks me. It offends me. Who knows? Would there have come a time when committing a gesture that made it difficult for Lopez to profit from people dying might have seemed necessary?

Absolutely.

But instead of the opportunity coming, Lopez went and changed the game. He murdered Richie.

They've got me all wrong.

I was just trying to help.

What if people see these videos online and in ten years want real-life killings brought to their living rooms.

Now, the only choice is to expose what we do before it's too late.

If they want to make me a commodity, that's simple, I'll un-commodify myself.

But what about the big picture?

Nipples is at the front of the bus staring at people.

What is he even doing?

Is he cleaning the glass with his T-shirt?

No, now he's licking it.

I love that kid.

How can I not love a kid who needs friendship so badly he'll do anything?

But he worries me.

Lopez's been paying him to train the new people, another one of his exercises in the ethics of cruelty.

Is it obvious to everyone else that Nipples is a twenty-four-year-old virgin?

A couple days ago he told Pebbles something about a dead girlfriend, a not-so-happy story, and the frontrunner of all my guesses as to why he came back.

He just wants someone to put him down.

20

THE OTHER ME

"GABRIEL? GABRIEL," THEN it all becomes a whisper, a real whisper, "Please, Gabe. Where are you right now? Talk to me."

"Lying in bed."

"But where?"

My response is I'm not telling.

This makes her sob.

It's even a little heartbreaking.

I go ahead and ask which airport she's visiting at the moment.

"Munich to Schipol and now I'm finishing a layover at Polkovo. That's in Russia. I've been calling you ten times a day all week."

She whispers again. Like she did the last time we saw each other. Her body a big black and blue, still in the hospital bed from punctured organs, a tight-jawed glare, her face ready to slide off because maybe she knew when

I said I was going down to the cafeteria for coffee and a grilled cheese she wouldn't see me anymore.

What is the sound of your sister's throat tightening to fight back tears in an attempt to speak?

"Why did you pick me, asshole?"

"Not sure what you mean. You sure you have the right number?"

"Tell me where you are. Something's happening to you. You need me."

"Don't need you."

"You need me, Gabriel."

"Don't."

"Yes. You do. Why are you talking like that?"

I smooth one hand over my thigh scar. Long and thick and purple.

"Don't you have a plane to catch?"

"I've got credit cards, and miles up the ass. Tell me what city and I'm there in nine hours."

"If what you believe in is true, then I'm with you now, because I'm a part of you, because I'll always be with you."

"That's not what that means," she tells me, then tells me how, "We need each other in the real way, you asshole."

"Need what? We're all just bodies. In a state of perpetual decay. We're just too in love with ourselves to realize that."

Cic' screams, "That's no kind of fucking argument!"

"Seriously though. How would seeing me in Gainesville, Ithaca, or Durham, wherever you think I may be, how is that any different from seeing a banana, or a peach?"

"It's a little more complicated than fruit."

"We're all just mortal fruit, Cicely. Yet we never think twice about taking a bite out of a peach and the suffering this causes."

"Fruits aren't people, fuck-bucket!"

"We think nothing of what the plum perceives: morally, emotionally or consciously."

"Would you tell me where you are if I said I'd renounced Buddhism?"

"No yes maybe. I don't know. What did you always tell me, you said, 'The idea of being separate is what makes us suffer. To stop suffering, we have to stop thinking about attachment and all that.' Right?"

"It all goes away. It all goes away once you accept everything without duality."

"Sorry, baby. Tried that. And all of it still feels pretty real."

A minute of silence, of airport static, Russian voices in mid-commute and the AC in my window vibrating against the sill before she pulls the old grieving card out and barfs, "I need my brother. I need the little boy who would crawl into bed with me every night because we were all we had. Can't you remember how that felt, how we could have just as easily been born the same person?"

"Don't milk the monoamniotic twin thing, darlin'."

"Don't you remember me kissing your forehead in the womb?"

"Sure."

"How about when I unwrapped the cord from your neck?"

"You shouldn't have."

"I saved you, you saved me. What's more important than that?"

"It's real sweet gushy stuff I wanna hold and squeeze, but baby, your bro croaked back in the Keys. You're the sole survivor."

Cicely's saying, "I picture you now and know it's nothing like what you see in the mirror every day. Do you ever do that?"

I close my eyes.

"The longer you run from what he did to you, the more it will never go away," she says.

"You keep buzzing around the planet," I tell her, "I'm sleepy." I press end to shush her protests and hear a knock at the door.

Fred's there with Wonkie, who's wearing an inside-out T-shirt, rubbing sleep from his eyes even though it's just past ten at night.

"You ready, Nipples?"

"For what?"

Ten minutes later Wonkie drops us off in front of a boat, which sits on a trailer in the driveway of a middle-class suburban home.

21

KILLING MORE PEOPLE

Wonkie kills his headlights a few houses down and parks curbside.

Fred motions for me to knock on the door to the houseboat once we're up the small set of stairs.

My personal trainer seems a little sleepy-eyed and folds his arms, even though he's not cold, he's just been just stabbed almost thirty times in the last year and a half and his body is slowly failing him.

The surgeon Wreck is waiting in the car with Wonkie and was instructed to enter the boat after the first genuine scream.

This means for surgery.

This means someone's going to get stabbed very soon.

After he swats a mosquito on the back of his neck Fred says to me, "All those Stella Adler classes you took are about to pay off."

He places his hand on my shoulder and squeezes, "Your motivation is to not get killed."

On the ride over Fred and Wonkie told me how Alex got a call from these Turkish guys that used to come to the living room a lot and now wanted a private viewing and were willing to pay us each four times the usual salary.

Alex's mere association with what's about to happen makes me regret leaving my motel room.

The man who opens the door is five-feet-two with newly whitened teeth.

He's wearing a silk seventies shirt with animal designs, unbuttoned to his belly, a lawn of short sweaty pubes on his chest.

Inside the boat is one small room with a leopard-skin rug and a tiger- striped couch.

What might be jazz but sounds more like a herd of elephants in a car wreck plays softly from somewhere.

Above the couch is a wall-sized painting of Las Vegas, while on the sofa sits a taller, wiry Turk wearing the same style clothing as his friend, his jaw a sideways seesaw, which might have something to do with the ant hill of pink cocaine clustered on the glass coffee table in front of him.

He says he's Senna, and that the guy who answered the door is his brother, Barak. Barak takes a seat beside his brother.

With a bored look Fred asks for the money please.

"Is no problem," Senna says with an open palm, then reaches under the couch cushion and tosses Fred two stacks of Jacksons, which he shoves down his waistline.

"So," Senna says with a shrug, "Time to be crazy guys, yeah?"

Fred smirks at me and tells me to remove my Army jacket.

He removes his denim one with great pain and pulls a T-shirt over his head that reads "Last Week's Abortion" with an arrow pointing up, revealing a bloody wrap-around chest-bandage.

Senna tells Fred it looks like he's been busy.

"You boys paying for a killing, aren't you?" he asks them, then asks me if I feel like killing him this evening, or if me dying is something I can live with.

Senna's laughing it up while Barak stirs a glass of bourbon with a coke spoon, sipping it like soup, un-amused.

"Put your knives away," says Senna. "We want you try something different."

Barak puts down his glass and from a small leather bag under the table, removes two chrome-plated six-shooters. Senna smiles.

Fred hands me one of the pistols.

"Fellas up for a little Polish Roulette this evening?"

"Polish? What is it?" Senna asks, licking his lips.

Fred smiles at the floor and tells them to watch, then opens the chamber of his pistol, removes four of the six bullets, closes the chamber, and spins.

The Turks laugh, then Fred puts the gun to his head and says, "Swallowing this takes seven years to digest," and me and the Turks scream, "Whoa! Fuck!" and that kind of stuff at the same time. After the click Fred hands me the piece.

"Polish Roulette. Crazy shit. Fuck my ass," Senna says, then asks me if I've got as much balls as my friend.

I'm faced with the idea of my brains splattering all

over the walls and floors of the Turkish porn kings over here who fit the profile of dudes who have tasted poop and smiled.

These are the folks who want more than anything to see my guts spill and hold them between their ass-smelling fingers in assessment.

These are addicts of horror and death, whose only redemption is at least they're honest about their fetish and don't indulge in it nightly with their televisions then shake heads pretending the world is going to shit and they can't stand to see it happen.

Those people want to say what is the world coming to when the world has really come to them.

My question to Senna and Barak is: "You want a little crazy?"

"Show me," Senna barks, punching the air, "show me the stupid crazy. I wanna gotta have it, man."

Fred sits on a plastic-covered recliner and scrapes some dirt from under his fingernail.

"You'd give anything to see me blow my brains across the mini-bar, wouldn't you?" I say.

"Yes! Yes!"

When Senna answers me is when my wrist jumps and slams the chamber closed.

Three bullets in my hand into my pocket means three left inside and the life expectancy of everyone in the room's shot down to a little south of usual.

"My game's not the same as his," I tell them, moving closer, "This one's called 'till you fuckin' die.'"

Fred says from the chair that this game is one of his favorites.

After the barrel finds its way into the mouth of Barak, Senna has no time to scream before the click and now the dark eye's on him.

And then another click.

Then back on Barak where I go and ask them if maybe I oughtta spin the chamber before – there goes another click.

And as still as the painting that hangs above them, Senna's recoiled against the back of the couch with his hairy arms covering his face while Barak's expression remains pitbull-tight as a black form blossoms on his tan slacks and down his leg.

"For God's sake, Nipples."

Senna asks me through choked tears and snot to please not pull the trigger again, because the one hundred percent odds he's got of becoming a piece of Abstract Art doesn't make him feel very lucky or happy inside anymore.

Cic' would say a tender act of mercy would be to just give someone you hate a warm and fuzzy hug.

"Fred," I'm saying, and Fred throws me his gun, knows my intentions like he knows every detail of this one-act play before it goes up.

My act of mercy to the Turks is to tell them not to worry, because we're still playing the same game.

Senna looks at Fred's revolver as if he's holding a strange child when I place it in his hands.

His palms are black with calluses.

I point my gun at Senna and tell him to point the gun he's holding at his brother.

His face tightens.

I tell him he wanted to see someone's brains blown out.

I tell him it's hard, isn't it, killing that which you love most in this world.

And that time heals nothing except what's on the surface.

"Please, man," he lunges forward and wraps himself around my knees, "Mercy. Okay? You can't live with it, crazy man."

"You big faker," I'm telling him, noticing a large tattoo of a dragon on his skull underneath the greasy black hair.

Barak eyeballs his brother's gun lying limp in his hands.

All I have to do is smile to see that idea dissolve and flicker out.

Mercy.

Sure, I think.

We could put all our guns down and have some drinks, snort some blow, laugh, cuss, maybe play a little Texas Hold 'em.

Who knows, we could end up going on fishing trips in Coos Bay, or flying out to Istanbul for the holidays.

Wear green sweaters and shit.

But the dream, it goes and dies when Fred peers over one of the magazines he's reading and informs me I might want to hurry up and end this game because, "Nipples," he says, "A man in an Alligator shirt just shimmied up that tree outside the window with a rifle he's not apt to miss with when he decides to fire upon one of our heads."

The loud hollow popping sound outside means Wonkie's seen this too from down the street.

Senna lets go of my knees and gazes up at me with the eyes of a baby and mouths, "Mercy. Mercy. Mercy."

"Fine," I say, taking Fred's pistol from Senna's slippery palms, "You got it," and see Fred's at the door now, urging me out with a cock of the head, followed by three more popping sounds outside and some screaming.

"Just one more thing," I lean in and whisper to Senna, "You have no clue what a guy like me can't live with."

Then I press the barrel into his thigh and squeeze the trigger.

22

GARBAGE

IT'S ME UP front and Wonkie driving to the Fill-Her-Up station to meet Alex and follow him out to some spot Wonkie says would be the best place to dispose of the man in the Alligator shirt, whose body is in the trunk.

We've pulled over twice for me to puke.

Fred and Wreck are behind us in the dead guy's Camry, which we found parked a few blocks away.

Wonkie doesn't have much to say and maybe this has something to do with Fred and me running out of the Turks' boat to find Wonkie stabbing the guy in the belly as Wreck hobbled over with a black medical bag.

Wreck said it's the fall from the tree that killed him, that the seven knife wounds were incidental.

Still, he tried to resuscitate him even while Wonkie bellyached how the fucker'd come to kill Fred for not returning Lopez's calls to see if Fred would do what he does in the living room some more so Lopez can sell the videos.

Then Wonkie stabbed the dead guy again.

Wonkie said Alex said Lopez said Fred is messing up everything Lopez is trying to do, such as kill and exploit the desperate and the disturbed for money.

He said Alex said Lopez called what Fred's doing downright immoral.

We pull over as Fred drops Wreck off at the same apartment complex I told Scar contained the hundreds of cells that were connected but not.

In my rearview, I watch the surgeon swagger into the lobby with his black medical bag and a sunken head. Poor little guy tried to revive Alligator shirt so many times, a gallon of blood shot out of the corpse's mouth like a whale spout.

Once we're driving again, Wonkie says, "That guy's more a priest than a doctor. Like everyone under his knife is his own family. What kind of way to live is that?"

We don't speak until we're under the neon halo of the gas station arch, waiting for Alex to show.

Fred parks behind us and kills the engine.

Wonkie smokes a lot of cigarettes and aims for the pumps when he flicks the butts.

Agnes curls from around the back of the building. She sees me glaring, but looks too cracked-out to notice.

With a raspy voice, I ask Wonkie if he'll buy me a bottle of water and get an abrupt no.

A few minutes later Alex's clunky green pickup pulls in beside us.

He leans over the passenger seat and rolls the window down. He asks Wonkie, "How many packages?" referring to the amount of bodies in the trunk.

Alex coughs a few times, then spits into some balled-up toilet paper.

"Just the one. Killer here went at him like he was a Turkish piñata."

"Where's the other brother?"

Wonkie shrugs, "You got the shovels?"

Alex pinky-points toward Snapper Creek Drive. Now we're all following the pickup.

The bumper sticker on Alex's tailgate says, "Back the Badge."

Fred told Wonkie earlier to lie about who's in the trunk so we can see Alex's reaction when we get to the Everglades and we take the real body out, then we'll know if Alex knew Fred and me were supposed to die on the boat.

We turn onto a dirt path twenty miles outside of Homestead, drive for a half hour, stopping again for me to puke, then off-road into the grass for another ten minutes until we reach the spot.

The spot is clearly the spot because through the high beams, I'm seeing at least ten legs sticking out of the ground.

This is Alex's graveyard, where he's been taking the people who don't survive the living room.

Fred told me Alex asked for this job, said one day Lopez's going to give him a special name, like The Mortician. Amidst the sounds of dying engines and slamming doors, I inch up close to a few of the legs, some half-stripped to the bone by vultures.

Tiny mosquitos fly into my eyes and nose.

Fred leans against the front of Wonkie's Cadillac, arms folded, his face the only darkened feature.

Alex is wearing a green hoodie. He shivers from the late-night drizzle.

He throws me and Wonkie shovels from the bed of his truck, taking one for himself, then hacks up into his ball of toilet paper before we begin.

It's clear by their speed and small talk about hunting knife manufacturers that I'm the only one digging his first grave.

I puke again.

Alex coughs, points at me and says, "Food poisoning."

"Stabbed his first dude," Wonkie says.

I puke some more. Coleman's face leers back at me in the orange puddle.

Twenty minutes later, we're over at the trunk of the Cadillac. Wonkie gives Fred a quick glance before we pop it. Now we're all watching Alex's bloodshot eyes as he sees the man with the Alligator shirt inside.

Wonkie's got his gun pressed to Alex's forehead, cocking the hammer as Alex hacks up a chunk of something colored-sounding and I'm covering my good ear and hurling on the exhaust pipe.

"You flirting with me, Wonkie?"

He says this like he's tired and wants to go home, like three of his friends called him up one night when he had the flu and asked him to help them get rid of a dead body.

Wonkie slams Alex's head on the edge of the trunk and jams the gun into the back of his skull, keeping him almost nose to nose with the dead man's frozen scream of a face.

Fred's squeezing Wonkie's shoulder only makes Wonkie angrier.

Alex says through strained laughter, "The offer was literally a thousand five. Set you two dumb-asses up with the Turks. Talked Lopez down to three hundred. Said it would be my pleasure."

Wonkie pistol smacks Alex, drags him around the side of the car and throws him into the fresh hole.

Then he reaches through the rear window, takes Fred's kerosene jug, pours it into the grave and feels his pockets for a match.

"Shit. All I got is a Bic."

Alex whistles from the grave and tosses him a Zippo.

I crawl alongside Fred over to the grave where the three of us watch Alex blow chunks of brain into his toilet paper hanky.

"What I'm gonna tell you?" he coughs some more, "This the part I lay down like a sack of shit. Beg for my life?"

"Keep talking," Wonkie says, lighting a dollar bill with the Zippo. "Be with you right quick. Literally."

"Self-righteous asshole. Half the bodies out here are yours. Buried 'em myself. Some of 'em still breathing."

"Wonkie only likes killing a little bit, Alex," Fred says, "But your addiction makes you their messenger."

"Do you believe half the shit that craps out your mouth?" Alex says.

Wonkie tosses the burning dollar into the grave, but it goes out before landing.

He stomps back over to his car. Something makes

me feel some action might be required on my part. I just don't know what.

Wonkie comes back over with an empty beer bottle, stuffing a few more bills in the top as he mumbles something about avenging Richie, although he doesn't use that word.

Alex mocks fierce applause and tells Fred, "They wanted to make you famous. You'd have been the spokesman of a generation. All for doing what you were doing already. Before you went all born-again."

Fred paces around the grave.

"We should all listen to Al. What kind of fool wouldn't take the reigns that were handed to him? Change lives, making everything he says and does a matter of world-shaping importance? And what better way to do that than by expressing our primal values, reaching people of all ages, creed and color, not through words, music or art, but through the flash of a blade. Could have been enough to make us all famous, and commodifiable: live-action trading cards of Nipples losing an ear. The Wonkie line of chocolate bars. The Dead Generation Christmas special. Dead because we'd provide the ultimate liberation from the powers we cannot change, so choose to accept. Dead because, if we could change them, those powers remain so deeply grooved in the great big brain, we'd never see a perceptible change in our lifetimes. Lopez found us all for different reasons. Maybe Wonkie needed to get in touch with his animal self in a way the animals he loves so much couldn't provide. Maybe Nipples just wanted to make friends, or go out the way he thinks he was supposed to. Could just be that Pebbles loved the sensation. Maybe they just never asked me to kill anyone worth killing. What about you, Alex? What's your excuse? And be honest, because our friend Wonkie's got a nose for horseshit, and much less forgiveness in his heart than me and Nipples, who would rather not watch you burn."

"Sorry Fred," Alex sinks his head, "'fraid with me, it all boils down to killing. Army wouldn't have me cause my feet are flat. Done too much acid to be a cop. I hate Lopez much as you. But I need him. It's those three to four seconds. After my knife crunches through. When the light in their eyes changes. For me it's magic. You fucking people. Like your shit don't stink. I'll make my mark. Get it all out in one big burst someday."

"Yeah you will, shit stain," Wonkie says.

Alex throws his hands up in mock surrender before saying, "Hey. Fellas. Lotsa luck with the revolution. Back when I was a kid, common knowledge was if you wanted to take down the house, you did it from the inside. That's what they taught at my school."

"What school was that?" Wonkie asks.

"The school of suck my balls."

Wonkie lights the bills in the bottle and lowers it for the toss.

Fred grabs his wrist and blows out the flame.

Fred whispers, "It's nothing personal. He hates everyone. Period. But he still wants to be respected. And now he thinks we think he's shit."

Wonkie whispers back that we do think this.

Alex won't look any of us in the eye as we carry the dead guy over to the hole and toss him in on the count of three, and starting with one, I'm seeing his life flash before me at one frame-per-second.

One: preacher's son. Amish country.

Two: drowning his infant brother in the bathtub.

Three: strangling his first and only boyfriend with speaker wire. Eyes going gray forever.

"You forgetting something?" Wonkie points to Alex.

"Hey Al," Fred says, "If we give you a pass on the whole setting us up to die thing, are you going to do something spectacular when you climb out of there?"

"Crawl out your own damn hole," Wonkie says and spits in the grave.

On our way out, Fred follows us again in the Camry, stopping a few hundred yards away from the gravesite.

He gets out and douses the car with kerosene.

After he lights the bottle with the bills and throws it through the back window, everything seems to turn into a slow-motion hero-shot of Fred walking toward us, the burning car exploding over his shoulder.

23

NATURE

ON THE BACK patio of Fred and Wonkie's tiny apartment in South Miami, you, Pebbles, Fred, Gretchen and Wonkie lounge on bean bags, along with Wonkie's Great Dane who's curled up by Fred's bare feet, staring out at the trees.

The dog growls when Gretchen rubs the back of Fred's neck because she can feel him thinking too hard, his eyes soldered shut ever since he plopped down and groaned from the wounds that seem ancient.

Pebbles throws a leg over yours as you ease into the beanbag.

She does this because your leg won't stop shaking.

You used to be the kind of guy who would look at the way Pebbles' pink hair falls over one eye, the fuzz lining her cheeks or the way her neckless shirt exposes just a taste of collarbone and start in with the visions of her being really sick and bedridden and left to your care in some rural cabin lit by the sunrise.

The method actor in you might imagine she was in a massive car wreck, trapped by metal as everything went up in flames and onlookers watched the fire spread as you leapt over wrecked cars and ripped the door from its hinges, lifting Pebbles to safety just in time.

The things you always wanted to get paid to pretend to do.

"What's up?" Pebbles whispers, "You gonna hurl again?"

Then you'd rub faces and touch lips the way you did with Betsy, before she was partially decapitated in front of you.

Pebbles rubs her pinky back and forth over your jeans where the scar on your thigh sizzles underneath.

She does this because now she knows, because you told her your story a few days after Bam Bam hightailed it.

You rub your pinky over hers even though the only girl you could ever have visions of again vanished and would carve your chest with sharpened steel sooner than she'd let you save her from a burning anything.

A beanbag away, Gretchen glares at you, a Blue Crate set to strike while Fred says with closed eyes that you really need to take a shower.

Wonkie sucks the rest of a Smoothie through a straw. He asks Fred if he has any thoughts on the whole Lopez is gonna have us all buried alive in the Glades in unmarked graves thing.

Fred's asleep within seconds, Gretchen curled up beside him with trembling eyelids.

Cic' would say when you reach perfect enlightenment, you can choose the moment of your death and just die.

You twist and pull a few eyebrow hairs and fall asleep to the sounds of Pebbles' faint snores vibrating on your chest, confusing them for the sounds of screams you hear when you have some quiet time, your own screams in there somewhere under the sounds of Coleman's blade arcing and slicing, and the smell of the ocean on that Florida Keys back road.

Anything to wake up.

24

DYING

IN THESE PRE-DAWN hours roaming an alley off US-1 with insomnia, the sounds of Pebbles's snoring reverberate in my skull.

Sometimes these alleys serve as gateways for what's left.

Inside the dumpster, I burrow, finding an empty tube of Pina Colada- flavored sex lotion in my hand, still sticky on the outside. The last time I thought about rubbing off a quick one was after the evening in my motel room with Darla.

After a few shakes to loosen the tube, I'm digging my hands through empty milk cartons, twist-tied litter bags and a jacket full of Chicken Chow Mein, reminding me what was left of my last meal as I puked all over the Everglades.

Just as my hands dip in to the coat is when the Chicken Chow Mein moves a little, then moves again, and after brushing aside a few banana peels and two boxes of disregarded crullers, there's no choice but to accept that the Chicken Chow Mein is not Chicken Chow Mein at all, the Chicken Chow Mein is a dog with most of its left side missing, and now its innards are refuge to the maggots.

Which means I've got to do something.

That something appears to be getting rid of the maggots.

Problem is, both my hands are covered in a thick coating of dumpster juice, something not entirely healthy to apply to a dog's intestines.

His heart pumps faster now, ready to jump out at me and the thing to do in this situation is act, because the dog, he doesn't want to die.

With two careful hands reaching under him, I lift him to my chest and close my eyes.

My mouth sucks out more maggots and spits, then does it again, and when my eyes open, the little creatures are nibbling on a tub of yogurt at my feet.

The dog looks back and forth from me to nothing, and it licks my waist a few times before its eyes roll back and its heart stops.

My eyes well up and it takes a really long time before I put him back where I found him and let the bugs and maggots do what they do because they love themselves more than us.

The tube of Pina Colada lotion sticks to my hand again.

Then a man's voice asks from behind me if maybe there's isn't a more discreet place to pleasure myself. He adds that there must be someplace, since I look too boyish and adorable for a bum's life.

When I turn around I see that this man's voice is no man at all, just a familiar pale-skinned girl wearing a sleeveless puffy jacket, with a broom in one hand and a scooper in the next.

The street sweeper's shoulder-length brown hair and neck so soft you can smell the soap.

"Why are you looking at me that way?' she goes.

I climb out of the dumpster, shaking some strawberry milkshake off my shoe.

She says, "Come here, come closer." A warm smile blossoms around her lips, and she licks her thumb to wipe off a smudge from under my eye.

After a few seconds she whispers, "So beautiful," then says, gazing at the pavement, "You're one of those can't-be-alone types, aren't you?"

She says, "But you've always been alone anyway."

I dig into my jeans pocket. I pull out a wrinkled hundred, the last of my money from the living room where Andrew Jackson died.

She sees it coming, says "You don't have to," but doesn't stop me from taking the broom and rolling the bill into her hand.

She says lean the broom and scooper against the wall and after I do, bites her bottom lip when she hears me tell her how it's not payment for anything, that really, she just needs to clean up and start over, forget about all the shit she's had to do.

It's not who she really is. I tell her I can see right

through her. I tell the street sweeper we're the same person.

Then she's pinning me against the concrete wall, tagged on both sides, and she covers my mouth with hers, moving her tongue in small strokes, as I try and match her rhythm, even though all I can think about is what the maggots made my mouth taste like, and why she doesn't care.

Then she's kissing my neck like she's trying to suck out my Lymph Nodes.

"You've never done this, have you?" she says. "Relax, I'll show you how."

She places both of my hands underneath her T-shirt, guides them around, tilts her head back, her mouth open, purring while my longest fingers graze her nipples.

Cic' would say, sex: what better way to affirm the lack of fundamental separateness?

Call it lightheadedness, a jump cut, because now our pants rest at our ankles, and I'm ass-deep in a cold puddle as she rubs against me from atop, saying, "It's a little bigger than I expected," before sliding me in with her hand, her walls grabbing me like a slimy handshake.

Cic' would say the desire to fulfill another's desires isn't necessarily a desire.

It's the heartfelt desire for them to feel happy.

Cic' would say this is called love.

She lifts my chin and says to never stop looking at her, as she moves herself up and down using my shoulders and for a moment it doesn't even matter who she is.

I'm watching my own reflection in hers, telling myself there's no difference between me and her, there's every difference, because she didn't take the money, she took the money, because I can love her the way none of the others do, even for a moment, I can't even kind of love anyone.

She says for me to cum. She wants me to. She wants to feel all of me inside her.

Eyes melting into hers, everything starts rising.

Cic' would say negative sex is self-centered sex, when you're only concerned about you.

"Let's have a child," I whisper, and wrap my lips around her throat, "Marry me," and she says she's ready, and now our bodies are the same body and when we cum her lips shake, then she opens her mouth as if to scream, holds it open and doesn't, just screams in silence, both eyes locked shut until we unclasp hands.

We sit like this for a few minutes, rocking back and forth, breath heavy.

The way she buries my head in her chest means she wants this moment to last forever. It means she can't be saved from the things she does, that a guy like me has to save himself first, and that maybe she doesn't even want saving.

I'm telling her I can love her if she'll let me.

And she holds me harder.

Relentless, "We can get out of here. Start over. Maybe it's not too late for either of us, you know?"

She says she knows. She understands me.

Then this idiot, this malignant slice of afterbirth says to her, "Whatever happens, you don't have to do this anymore."

That's when her grip loosens and she looks at me

with her chin down, eyes half shut and says, "Do you feel it yet?"

As I lean in to kiss her, she spits laughter, covers her mouth, turning wagon-red.

"What? What's funny about that? Let me fucking help you."

This makes her laughing turn to heaving then turn back to laughing until she breathes in deep, breathes out, and lets her face sink back into all sweet and loving.

She says, "Come here, I want to tell you something."

Leaning forward, turning my head and resting it on her shoulder, she rolls the one hundred-dollar bill into a ball and slides it deep into my pocket.

Then she strokes my hair and whispers, "You just got AIDS, motherfucker."

She waves bye-bye and giggles.

She laughs her pants back on.

Laughs her broomstick and scooper into her hands, and cracks herself up down the alley until there's no more laughing, just bristles on pavement.

What is the sound of your life ending one garbage scoop at a time?

25

THE BLACK RHINO

"Wanna know my personal tragedy: people who like to pick on the little guy, namely man-tittied husbands in golf shirts who talk down to their wives in diners and get pleasure out of making them feel like doody."

"I know what you're going to say. 'You're not welcome to sit at our table and this is not a golf shirt, young man, it's a Polo.'"

"But it is a golf shirt. It's a golf shirt even when you're naked."

"Thing is, makes the hair on my arms stand up introducing myself like that."

"Used to mean something else."

"See, you sitting here at this table criticizing your lovely wife, it's the kind of thing people call: going about your business."

"Maybe sometimes folks look over at you all shifty, stirring their soup or looking at watches they're not wearing, and in some ways, you're like their invisible marriage counselor, 'cause you make all the husbands look good, and all the wives grateful."

"Which might save your life if you possessed a shit crumb of awareness about how others perceive you."

"But you don't."

"That's why today, it means your ass."

"See that?"

"Do-you-see-that?"

"The way your face almost slid off your skull when I said it means your ass?"

"That's 'cause everything between us just changed, right? Yeah? Look at your wife."

"Don't cry, all right? It's me: Wonkie."

"Don't know me?"

"I promise, that won't be a problem after today."

"'cause every time you wake up and feel that great weight – sorry, guy - lifted, and all of a sudden you have a life where what you think and believe in and care about is of major significance, and no big-and-tall suit-wearing slob tries to gaslight you into submission, this is the face you'll see smiling back at you."

"Don't stand. Please. Don't stand for that."

"Calm down, don't worry, it's just a Kasumi Sashimi cutlery knife."

"It's just the sharpest knife in the world."

"Nice to look at, I know it. Take a look. Go ahead. Hold it."

"No, okay."

"I bought this my freshman year in college."

"This surprise you?"

"Half Cuban redneck like me with an education: hair

all matted, wearing shorts and an undershirt and mountain boots, beer breath and a knife in your face."

"See that guy sitting at that table in the corner, with the cute little pink-haired girl and the darker chick leaning on his shoulder looking not so happy?"

"What, you blind or something, tittie man?"

"Entire place just ran out the door except them three."

"Good-looking guy with the jean jacket, looks like someone but you can't say who?"

"You believe we've been friends since first grade?"

"He came to live with my dad and me after his own dad shot and killed his whole family, even the dog."

"He's got a degree in Comparative Religion."

"Not me though."

"Just a Bachelors in Zoology."

"Maybe if my personal tragedy were the same as his, I'd want to learn about all the Gods too, find out which one let it happen, and slice him up."

"Well, almost got my Bachelors. I dropped out my second term."

"Spent a few years on the road, even drove through Europe a little, Northern Africa, picked up some tongues, a little Spanish, little Italian, all kindsa Russian."

"I can stab a mother fucker in twenty-six languages."

"What people say and how they say it's always fascinated me."

"But in the end, I missed them."

"Them who? The animals, who."

"They're my companions, my best friends besides the guy I just pointed out."

"You know how some folks, you might have heard

them say like, 'I really want a monkey? How cool would that be, bring a monkey to parties, a loveable chimp or one of those cute little things used to take pennies out your hand at county fairs?'"

"But they're never willing to put in the time."

"You pretty much have to dedicate your life to it. So yeah, I went through the classes, the training, all the clocked hours."

"Time I was eighteen I had a chimp and three Velvet Blackface's running around my dad's living room."

"Drove him ape shit. Ha!"

"Alice, that was my chimp, was a thrower."

"She's dead now."

"Speaking of which, you're gonna need this."

"It's not as well-crafted as my Kasumi."

"But it's titanium."

"Just leave it in front of you, keep it pointed sideways."

"No, sideways, not sideways pointed at me."

"There you go."

"Just leave it."

"And come on now, Titties, stop sweating so hard, thing's gonna slide right out your mitt come game time."

"And it's coming. Real soon, it's coming."

"It's like this, Titties: it's not so personal. All right?"

"Think you're the only omelet-eating slob acts like a cock to his wife in public?"

"Think I singled you out?"

"Can you be realistic for just one minute please?"

"You picked me, don't you think?"

"Not even your fault and don't pretend for a second I blame you for any of this.

"You're unlucky."

"I believe you don't know any better, all right, okay, I even believe you have no idea you're being rude to this woman, and that you would die for her if put to the test, I know it, so let's leave it at that, all right?"

"You picked the wrong diner this morning is all."

"You picked the wrong diner and you picked the wrong diner on a day that happens to be very important for reasons you're likely not to be around to fully understand when it's over."

"And it's almost over."

"We're getting there."

"If you feel like you're being treated unfairly, I'll go right-handed."

"I'm a southpaw."

"But I'll do that for you."

"And I'll do it on your mark."

"I promise you this: I, Juaquin Hill, will not take the first swipe."

"Unless you fuck around and do nothing for ten minutes and then I'll just carve you up where you sit, in a way it'll take another ten minutes to die from."

"I'm trying real hard to be the good guy here, Titties."

"I'll do it all for you."

"I'll do it, for the Black Rhino."

"See, I believe we all have an animal self."

"Black Rhino's yours."

"Sometimes people call it a dark side."

"Whoa. Spooky right?"

"I don't think so."

"I think that's all a bunch of horseshit, myself."

"Don't you, Titties?"

"There is no dark side and even if there was, calling it evil or mean is a pretty provincial attitude in my opinion."

"It's the part of ourselves that bears the brunt of all the fucked up shit we do even though we know it's wrong."

"It's nothing more than, how do you say it, it's nothing more than a well of badness that fills up so high we think to give it an identity, and wink at our reflections because we've come to believe this side of us that we call dark makes us interesting, mysterious, when it doesn't, it makes us liars, makes us justify ourselves to ourselves."

"The animal self is different. It's a natural part of us."

"Who knows, maybe real animals, they have people-selves."

"All I know is we're born with it."

"Guy over at the table I pointed out a minute ago, who looks asleep, he's a female mountain lion."

"Takes care of his young, remains calm and poised unless threatened, even though his human side's made him think he's better off letting himself be attacked."

"I've even stabbed him."

"Two times. Count 'em."

"Guy gets stabbed so he can save people from him stabbing them."

"He calls it 'Cool Anger,' some Eastern shit, don't ask me, told you, he's got the degree."

"Whatever helps him sleep at night."

"If he's the lion, we're his cubs."

"My animal's a Black Panther."

"No, not like that."

"It's actually a leopard, but that's a whole other discussion."

"Fierce, but calculating, always aware of my surroundings, trim and muscular, slipping like dark vapor through trees and vines, with blade-sharp insight into the actions and thoughts of others."

"Quiet by nature, but only because it always carries its power with fierce grace, and every panther uses its power differently: some to destroy, some to protect and some to bring honesty and wisdom into the minds of others."

"You could say I'm all three of those wrapped up in one."

"And today it just so happens all the animals are coming out."

"Listen, Titties, you gotta ask your wife—nicely!—to please stop crying."

"It's distracting my train here, man."

"Ma'am if you want, go wait in the bathroom, or go on outside, fuck it, I'm sure policemen have been summoned."

"Go on."

"Don't forget your purse."

"I knew you wouldn't say bye to her."

"We're sitting here for a while now and I've gone out of my way to make you one hundred percent aware of what's happening, even talked you through it, offered to handicap myself some and comes time for her to get out of our way and let us do our shit, you can't even take her hand, say you love her, say you're sorry or nothing."

"You, look at me Titties, you, only care, about your own self."

"Well now she's free of you."

"Stop crying."

"She's free of you."

"God damn."

"You see all those folks huddled up outside the window so they can get a peek at us getting down to business?

"She ain't there is she?"

"You know why?"

"'Cause she's running around like she's gotta pee real bad trying to get someone to come save your fat ass."

"But we both know that isn't gonna happen, don't we?"

"Now, sit up straight, stop slouching."

"Atta boy."

"Put both arms on the table, but grab one of those napkins first and wipe off."

"Right. There you go."

"Close your eyes and take a few deep breaths, try and imagine a cool mountain morn... all right, doesn't matter, forget it."

"Don't even think about running, Titties, I can smell you thinking it and you know as well as me it ain't your destiny."

"So let's go out with some dignity?"

"All right?"

"Now, take those breaths and not too deep because I don't want you hyperventilating on me."

"Don't pay any attention to my friends over there

watching, they'd just as soon see you pull through this and make an example out of me."

"They only look like they're made of wax."

"Those masks are masks of their own faces, same as ours."

"Same as the guy outside with the camera pointed at us. You see him?"

"Guy with one ear missing all nasty looking?"

"See, and now this is important, what's about to happen here ain't about you and me."

"It's about exposing this whole thing to the world and putting an end to it."

"It's about becoming the thing you want to destroy."

"Look, if it's any kinda comfort, chances are real good I'll be seeing you over at wherever you're going before sun up."

"All right then."

"Folks outside are wanting a show."

"Let's make some noise, Titties."

26

ALL KINDS OF CRAZY

THEY WAKE ME up in the middle of a morning nightmare, in the alley where the street sweeper left me.

The sun's beaming into my puffed-up eyes. All of me is sticky. It could be any day of the week. Kuba taps the butt of a hunting knife on my skull. The Beak stares down at me with his arms folded.

The Beak says, "Fred's out on the street taking knives in his chest. Pebbles and Wonkie went and sliced up four dudes already and it ain't even ten o'clock."

Kuba shakes his head when The Beak says this, which means it really isn't ten o'clock yet.

"Problem is the investor already heard about it on Twitter, which means he's probably pulling out."

For some reason I flash on the investor pulling a knife out of Lopez.

The Beak adds, "If Fred's trying to upset everyone, it's working. Shit needs to stop though. I got mouths to feed."

All that manages to come out of my mouth in response

is a few chunks of whatever I ate from the dumpster last night, blowing it all over Kuba's leather sneakers.

"Listen up: Lopez has a job for you, all right? You got an hour to find your boys, do what you gotta do to get them off the streets before the cops go on and do it for you. Do this shit, and Lopez say he's willing to forget all about the Turkish clients, and your role in this shit. Plus a one way ticket wherever you wanna go, and a stipend. Do this shit, and The Handle ain't gonna get involved with you."

The Beak lifts me up.

Tensing his jaw, trying to keep his chin up high, he grins. "All Kindsa Crazy."

The Beak's phone rings.

There's no greeting.

The Beak's expression turns to candle wax.

On his Facetime screen, casa de la Lopez is on fire.

27

PEBBLES

COP CARS BARREL while sirens scream as these boots kick dust. I shake off the sleep then clickety-clack across Kendall Drive, where a crowd forms around two figures blocking traffic.

The pink-haired girl wearing the black sweatpants and the lavender tank-top doesn't look at me when I stand at her side, just whispers, "Look at his face. Look how he wants to kill me. "

Everyone's filming Pebbles and the other guy and now me.

A few feet away, round, brown and bearded, Scar wears a long white T-shirt and shorts that come down to his chubby ankles.

His knife sits snugly in his waistline.

Beside me now, a middle-aged black guy with his arms folded and a pouty expression, wearing a grease-splotched chef's apron.

I'm saying to the chef, "Where you cooking at?"

"Excuse me?" he says, confused. "I'm a baker," he tells me, "Over at the Planet Cupcake."

He points at a strip mall.

"You use non-stick pans or the stainless-steel kind?"

"Why?" he says.

"Used to cook myself," I'm saying.

This chef laughs with a squinch of the eyes and a lick of the lips, looks away when he asks me, "Why are you trying to sound black?"

He's got a patched salt-and-pepper beard and a pink burn that covers most of his neck.

Two fire trucks wail from far off, scorching toward Lopez's exploded house.

Scar asks me how that brain percentage thing's been going for me.

"Going good," I tell him, deepening my voice a few more octaves.

"You got my back?" I ask the chef.

The chef steps off into the crowd of cell phones.

Scar takes the knife out of his waist and presses it against my face, which makes some of the crowd make noises.

"That ain't fair, yo."

Scar head butts my eye. I'm crawling into the crowd as Scar yells after me, "Fool, they're paying three thousand a head for you people. When I'm through dicing up this skinny, E.T.-looking bitch, you best pick the knife up out her dead hand."

Some people in the crowd help me up and brush me off.

The rest of them froth at the eyes and jowls with the promise of some good street killing.

I gaze at Pebbles for a sign, but there's only her throat moving and her fist tightening around the blade handle.

The way they did things in the Old West, narrowed eyes and fingers wiggling at the ready is how it really is.

The sounds of southern dust blowing and saloon doors swinging have been updated by car horns and ring tones.

Thick lines on Pebbles' forehead, pace of breath a beat too quick, licking the sweat above her lip, all these things are things Fred says give your opponent away.

And when you see them doing things like this, or the light of confidence leaving their eyes, a simple chin-crinkle, you know you can raise the blade, because there's no way you're going to lose.

Fred says he often does these things on purpose to boost his opponent's self-esteem.

Scar doesn't do this.

Scar criss-crosses his blade at the shoulder and comes at her like a baby bull.

Pebbles winds back and wings her knife and the thick streaks of blood pouring from his eye are a lifetime of tears.

Pebbles' phone vibrates. She stares at it.

"Wonkie says come to the Monkey Jungle."

"What's the Monkey Jungle?"

"It's a zoo, just for monkeys."

The crowd moves in, filming Scar's body as the sirens grow fainter.

28

ANIMALS

A BAND OF small white monkey's with orange Mohawks jumps, screeches and claws at tourists and security guards outside The Monkey Jungle.

They're all freaking out when me and Pebbles pull up to the entrance in the Jetta Pebbles carjacked.

Mostly the monkeys are freaking out.

A fat Cuban security guard comes right at us with a baton and a radio.

"Get back in the car please. Ma'am, ma'am put down the knife."

A wet and moist sound followed by stifled hacking as Wonkie pulls the blade out of the back of his neck and takes his place.

Wonkie stalks toward Pebbles and me, bloody knife hanging down at his knees. He glances both ways, cursing, the front of his undershirt several shades of crimson.

Across the street, white monkeys leap back into the trees.

Wonkie beckons us into the park, a little out of breath.

"I texted you because we need to free the animals."

"Fuck the animals," Pebbles tells him. "We're all getting killed today."

"That's why we need to free them. The monkeys. When we die, who will?"

Pebbles asks him if he heard about the fire.

"It has recently come to my attention," Wonkie says, "that Alex entered the living room at ten o'clock this morning, taped Lopez to a chair, doused the place in kerosene, cracked a beer, and lit a match.

Wonkie says it's over.

He says we can go home now, or do whatever we do when we're not doing this.

"What's with the monkeys?" I'm asking.

"Sort of a Harpers Ferry kind of thing. I had to stab four guards. Freed 'em all, I think. Except the baboons."

"Where's Fred?"

"Fuck Fred. This is about the baboons. Now come on, Wonkie chuckles, "It's a jungle in there."

Now Wonkie stops chuckling and motions across the street with a cock of his chin, where, oblivious to oncoming cars, The Handle strolls toward us in a three-piece suit, briefcase in hand.

29

BLOODLETTING

Imagine an SUV filled with six college friends and an older bearded stranger, cruising down a back road one spring night in the Florida Keys, waiting for him to give directions to his boat.

No lights and no other cars for miles.

Just the sounds of the engine blowing by, the creatures in the woods, a squirrel's head bobbing up with wide darting eyes.

In the back seat with three of them, the stranger palms a hunting blade, waiting.

His black beard covers the pockmarks and thick lips, the creases from his fatherly smirk.

Only the deep-set gray eyes light his face, harboring the screams of those he's ridden in the backs of trucks with before, always in packs of the weak.

Deep in The Monkey Jungle, Wonkie's released every brand of primate.

A Spider Monkey follows him as he double-checks the cages.

When Coleman brought forth the blade and buried it handle-deep in my thigh, it felt like he'd punched me, and it was hard to tell if he was joking or not, especially after the acid and the three vodka cranberries at the sandbar.

Everyone wanted to be sure it was real before they screamed, and by the time it started, the swings of his blade were wild, slicing without method.

In my mind, Coleman never opened his eyes, because the knife was not an extension of him.

For him, this was the purest form of living, which made him completely one with the blade, so it swung where it pleased.

He was almost no longer even in the car.

My eyes filled with Cicely's blood, sliced once in the arm, and twice below her left breast.

Justin died quickest, crawling into the back seat to protect us.

The first strike of the blade carved across his face, cutting off his nose.

His brother Sy took two slices on the back of his neck before Coleman lodged it all the way in.

The last thing Sy saw were the sparks flickering from his brother's eyes before plowing into the woods and sending the truck into a roll.

One of the cream-colored mohawked monkeys hisses when I jog past him, a fanged snarl as strings of some sort of cheese drip from its jowls, reminding me of Gretchen for some reason.

I yell for Pebbles.

At the entrance, The Handle stares in several directions before opening his briefcase and removing two medieval daggers with round ridges on the sides.

Wonkie whistles at him from the next corridor.

"You're gonna answer for Richie. Middle of the jungle, crazy man, that's where you'll find me."

The Handle leaves his briefcase by the entrance and heads for another walkway.

Right now, I don't even remember why I'm here.

"Wonders of Nature: Lemurs," Pebbles reads.

Her pink hair blows back as she sprints toward a far off exhibit.

Engine steam sifts from the overturned SUV.

Two are dead and Elizabeth screams as Coleman sends his dripping blade through her side like cake.

With each pass, her cries get louder, like the taste of her blood and her organs ripping fills her more with life.

When the screams stop, she's frozen in mid-agony, her eyes gone white from fear.

Still breathing: Coleman, Cicely, Betsy and the corn-fed dipshit shielding her with his useless scrawny ass, everyone resting for an indeterminate amount of time.

I stop running because Wonkie's propped against the inside of an open Plexiglas cage, as his chest blossoms a new shade of red. He begins his slow slide, leaving a smeared ribbon on the glass that tracks the exactness of his graceful collapse.

Maybe dying in the cell of those you freed are the best last words you're gonna get.

Cut to me stalking toward Pebbles as she waits on a wooden bridge overlooking a lagoon.

All the chimps are watching us.

The knife in her hand is one big blood drip.

"You know the thing about chicks with knives?" Pebbles says.

"What?"

"You'll turn around, walk away, and it won't hit you until you're in the parking lot that you've even been stabbed.

Now a sudden sting on my ear, and the slice of air. When I touch my ear with my fingers, I feel the lower half dangling. A small tug and I'm holding it.

The ringing in what's left of my good ear is what mutes my scream is what makes me drop it, then kneel and try to pick up the chunk and on my way back up notice the back of Pebbles's lavender shirt blooming with blood.

I reach for her as the force of the Handle's knife goes in again and lifts her off the ground and over the railing.

She's twisting her body all the way around, and with the other hand thrusts her knife straight at him, almost like an offering as she falls and the confusion in her eyes more than anything else makes me turn my head in fear.

I stare at the backs of my eyelids and when I open them, The Handle's sitting propped against the railing and he's clutching his hand to the spot on his throat where Pebbles' knife went in, pools of blood coming out like milk, but his expression hasn't changed, so he doesn't appear to be in any pain even though I swear his soul's bouncing off the trees and the rocks, like Pebbles let all the air out of a large, black psychopathic balloon.

The Handle's lips are moving, but I can't hear a thing.

His glass eye glares long after his breath stops.

In the lagoon, two chimps nudge Pebbles as the mother breastfeeds with pulpy eyes.

30
NECK

THIS IS SUPPOSED to be the part where I head off into the sunset, like a wide shot of me slow walking out of The Monkey Jungle, oblivious to the barrage of cops and people in Animal Control windbreakers sprinting past me with rifles and tranquilizer guns, to the muted horns and noiseless helicopters overhead, and the world's most exotic monkeys running amuck.

Up ahead the street's barricaded. Three guys stand off in triangle formation, surrounded by a larger crowd than before, more cell phones filming.

Two of them repeatedly stab the third guy until he falls down.

I pick up the pace as Kuba and The Beak pocket their blades and take off in opposite directions amidst massive applause.

Fred's not moving so I nudge him with my sneaker.

He pulls himself into a sitting position and the clapping of the spectators gets louder as he forces a smile through a sharp ray of sun glint and coughs up a few strings of lung.

He sits with his arms folded around his knees, staring at the pavement.

I help him to his feet, where he wipes some blood from my cheek and speaks even though no words are coming out because The Handle's knife went and put the world on mute.

Fred might be saying, "What makes us the same right now is all my friends are dead too."

He's staring at my feet, telling me things. Then he leans in, sniffs me and says, "When did you contract HIV?"

Then she's there. Already through the crowd and coming our way. Comfort's knife dangles in her hand. Eyes locked on Fred. The same outfit from before.

"Step back, Nipples." With a gentle palm on my chest, he gives a light push.

You're propping yourself on the caved-in door of the SUV, reaching a tentative hand through the passenger-side window you just crawled out of, calling out to your girlfriend.

The wounds in your ribs and left leg remain in the numbing stage.

"Betsy," you whisper, because you don't want to risk disturbing the dead, don't want the wolf inside to wake and hear you.

After a couple of tries she tweaks her head and her eyes open. She's the only one who hasn't been stabbed or wounded, the triple flip and crash against the tree notwithstanding.

A fresh rush of energy makes you reach your arm through the window and tell her to grab your hand.

It takes her a few tries to push up into a kneel and then you've got her and you're pulling her up now.

She slips, but you hoist with animal strength because you know she's going to make it now, this red-haired angel who wakes and strokes your face with the back of her hand making the tips of the hairs on your spine rise, makes it feel the way you always knew it would if any of the ones from preschool until now had even given you a chance in hell to show them how to love you back.

She clasps her small hands on the edge of the window frame and you've got her with one tug easy, but then you catch a fresh set of eyes trying to reach yours and they're eyes you've known since long before your births and catching the pain and cherry-colored tears running down your sister's face, you reach for her too.

It takes a slow second for Cicely to grab your other hand and help you help her to the window, where now she's gazing up at you a little south of Betsy.

Then Coleman's climbing up from the shadows of the inner wreckage.

He's got the blade to Cicely's throat and her hair pulled back taut, and now it's pressed against the side of Betsy's neck and she, as if trying to make it easier, like she's in on it, cranes her neck back and turns into the sharpness of it, eyes glazed and lips twitching.

Coleman never looks at them. His eyes never leave yours. The low wind makes what he's saying a low grumble. Cicely's losing control of her breathing. The whites of her eyes show. When you look at Betsy, Coleman shifts along with you. His face never flinches as he strokes Betsy's cheek with tender fingers. You ask Coleman to do whatever he's going to do to you instead.

Coleman smiles and says he can see it happening to you already and that you shouldn't let it yet, because you still have to choose, and by giving you this choice, he's making you one with God, which means he's giving you control of the universe, over everyone in it, making you one with them in a way you may never again experience, and what you do with this gifting, that's another choice altogether and it's harder than the one you're about to make.

With both hands you pull on the girls' arms.

He tightens his grip. Coleman says he'll let you have one of them.

When you beg in incomplete sentences you know he's done this before because he inhales with closed eyes, taking in the denial in your chest and tells you with delicate resolve it's not up for debate.

He says we can do both of them, so don't try and reason with this because this here is real now and there's no way you're getting out of it.

When he says this, he moves the blade back and forth from Cicely's neck to Betsy's.

His werewolf grin and dead eyes smell every thought, everything you're trying to do to make this stop.

He twirls a lock of Betsy's hair between his fingers and pulls, puts it in your hand.

The way you remember things, it was the glossy eyes of both girls watching you and Coleman's black and silver bearded face sunk low as a street dog's, red over the whites of the eyes, even though you're sure you couldn't have looked at any of them, at least not in a way you were really choosing.

Coleman said something that made you think he might have loved you.

It was the tenderness, the way your father's voice sounded when he put you on your first tricycle and had you pedal toward him in the courtyard of the apartment complex, his arms open, black leather jacket hanging onto his skinny bones.

But it was Coleman's voice saying, "You're almost there. Keep one foot forward. Whatever you do, kiddo, don't step backwards."

That's when you hoisted Cicely by her soaked underarms and placed her on the dirt before reaching back for Betsy too, but the noises made you turn away and jump off the truck where you and Cicely propped each other up.

All you pictured was how it might have happened in reverse, Coleman sinking smoothly into the darkness of the truck, then the sawing of the knife, the last image of her you allow yourself not to forget.

Fred tries to embrace Comfort when she swings, putting the knife in his neck.

The crowd scatters for safety, some climbing onto the roofs of parked cars.

One woman winds back around the open door of her SUV like a centipede.

Comfort buries her knife in his heart and Fred's eyes remain smiling up at the sky.

She walks away as if nothing happened.

I do the same.

31

ROLLOUT

PEOPLE WHO BELIEVE in that kind of crap think when folks die, they get straight-up recycled, and go around telling themselves they were once Cleopatra or George Washington.

But maybe it means something else.

We're constantly exchanging energies, taking on aspects of one another. All we are made up of are other peoples' chunks of self.

When you die, your energy scatters and merges, but when you're alive, it's doing the same thing, just in smaller stages.

We're all dying every second.

The constant is that there's no constant at all.

People who rigidly cling to who they think they are, they're missing out.

Cic' would say this, and I would agree with her crazy ass.

How I got here is a complete mystery.

The only things I remember are tiny shards of seconds, images and subliminal cuts of stuff that might or might not have happened over the course of the last three days.

Do I remember kicking in the sideboards at the base of my motel room bed?

I do not.

How about crawling under here and staring at the back of my mattress spring for seventy hours without eating or drinking and letting what needed to come of me come out of me?

None.

Cic' would say don't think about old shit. She'd say you have to live in the moment.

But what if the moment sucks?

Subliminal cuts. Timeless flashes freeze framed in my brain.

Like Gretchen reaching under the bed and pummeling me harder screaming, "You fucking killed him!" then finding her way under the bed and into my arms.

Jump cut to the surgeon Wreck on the other side, reaching under the bed with a small flashlight between his teeth, the smell of whiskey as he stitches my ear back together.

Finding my cell phone wedged in my fingers, the puddle beneath me cold with each shift of my hips.

It took somewhere between three seconds and a day-and-a-half to ring.

Everything Cicely said on the phone, I probably sighed and gave in.

The cab ride to Miami International Airport is a

thin black blur of police barricades, pockets of exhaust, a suicidal bird impaling itself on the wiper blade and the pencil the driver uses to pry it off.

I stand in the spot where The Beak found me.

In a few minutes my sister will run out from her gate and hug me with juicy eyes.

This is the part where Agnes walks by and smiles with a tooth missing.

The Beak drives past in his van with his eyes gleaming as he eats half a cheeseburger, on his way to arrivals.

The street sweeper scooping garbage in the distant background.

Crane up as I throw my arms in the air in triumph.

Pull back further and further, until we're so small the clouds move over us.

Until the score darkens and the narrator's voice says: "Together we can be a person again."

"One very fucked up person."

"It will be like nothing ever happened."

As a plane flies across the frame and we roll credits.